PRO SE PRESS

NIGHTVEIL: CRISIS AT THE CROSSROADS OF INFINITY
A Pro Se Productions Publication

Written by Bobby Nash
Editing by Bill Black and Ernest Russell

Cover by Bill Black
Book Design by Antonino Lo Iacono & Marzia Marina
New Pulp Logo Design by Sean E. Ali
New Pulp Seal Design by Cari Reese

Pro Se Productions, LLC
133 1/2 Broad Street
Batesville, AR, 72501
870-834-4022

editorinchief@prose-press.com
www.prose-press.com

CONTENTS

1.

At the edge of infinity, chaos reigned.

Explosions of colors bloomed in a miasma of intricate patterns all around her. The colors were far more vibrant than she had ever seen naturally occur in nature or created by man.

If not for the dire circumstances behind the phenomenon, the sorceress would have found it all quite beautiful, spectacular even. However, circumstances being what they were, the danger lurking behind the beauty was difficult to ignore. Whatever caused the disaster unfolding all around her, her senses told her it was not a natural occurrence.

Someone did this deliberately! Someone caused this on purpose! But how?

Knowing more than a bit about how the realm magicks work, the sorceress was only one of a handful who could truly understand the ramifications of the chaos created all around her. Whoever was responsible, their power was great. It would take an extremely powerful mystic to pull off anything on this epic of a scale.

That limited the number of possible suspects considerably, down to only a handful at best. She personally knew a couple of entities powerful enough to even dream of accessing this amount of raw, unfettered power, much less control it. She counted herself among that list, though she couldn't fathom ever trying to tap into the magicks it would take to pull off something of this magnitude.

The enemy was bold, brazen, and powerful.

The sorceress called forth her own magicks and prepared herself for battle. A lime green force screen sparkled to life around her then quickly faded from view.

Now protected by the defense screen, she pressed on.

Before her, separated only by a mystical barrier, the interdimensional vortex that surrounded the Crossroads of Infinity raged. Strings of lightning-like energy bucked and heaved along the outer spiral, chipping away bursts of energy from the barrier and sending them off into the ether. There was no end to the danger they would wreak wherever they landed.

What the hell is causing this? the sorceress wondered.

The vortex was never what you would call calm, but she had never seen it this bad. It threatened to spin out of control.

This was not her first time crossing the matter streams that surrounded the interdimensional vortex, the barrier between realities. Traversing the Crossroads of Infinity was no easy feat, but with her powers, she had managed it on a few occasions. Appearances to the contrary, the barrier was not solid. No solid object could contain the great vortex. The barrier was an energy field, constantly fluctuating to keep the vortex spinning in place as its tendrils weaved their tapestry throughout all of the parallel and unconnected dimensions.

The barrier surrounding the Crossroads of Infinity was one of the greatest unsolved mysteries of the multiverse. No one knew who constructed the barrier or how, but there were many who had dedicated their lives to find the answer.

So far, none had been successful.

With careful planning and skilled manipulation, someone who knew how to wield the same magicks as she did could slip between the fluctuations and safely cross over to the other side of the barrier into a neighboring dimension. It wasn't easy, but it could be done. She, herself, had traversed to alternate worlds on more than one occasion.

In none of her previous visits to the wasteland had the vortex ever looked anything like it did now. The wasteland surrounding the interdimensional nexus was normally peaceful, quiet, serene.

The opposite of how it appeared to her now with its surface cracked and burnt.

Though never calm, the vortex was more like a thunderstorm on a warm summer's day rather than the tumultuous scene she witnessed. What spun before her now was more like ten force five hurricanes stacked one atop the other as they made landfall. Solar winds pushed against her as she approached, threatening to knock her out of the sky, but she managed to keep her bearings.

The colors were spectacular, but also disturbing as the explosions of the spectrum assaulted her senses and threatened to overwhelm her. She could feel the pressure behind her eyes threatening to trigger the mother of all migraines. It was almost more than the heroine could bear.

Azagoth, protect me, the sorceress thought as she pushed forward. It had been a long time since she had muttered her former mentor's name, even longer since he answered, but with the overwhelming chaos around her, thinking of Azagoth helped calm her a bit.

Bursts of temporal energy erupted nearby, throwing time and space out of synch. The phenomena wasn't only relegated to the wastelands at the edge of known space, but the chaos had reached all the way back to her home world of Earth as well.

It had started off small, as these things are wont to do. Reports of ghosts were the first indicator that something was off. Loved ones long thought dead showing up for their old jobs or coming home for a family meal. After the initial shock wore off, the reunions became a blessing to those who got one last chance to talk with their loved ones before they disappeared back to wherever they had been before.

Then there were roads that suddenly went in different directions than normal, taking travelers to odd destinations. New neighborhoods popped up in cities around the world. All of these things were vexing, but nothing that caused any irreparable harm.

Time, it was believed, had come unstuck, non-linear.

It wasn't until a stampede of long-tailed dinosaurs that had been long thought extinct started marching down Miami's main drag that curiosity turned deadly. The sorceress leapt into action as soon as she saw the news report of the Jurassic convoy making its way down Interstate 95.

After corralling the lost fossils where they would not be able to do any permanent damage, the sorceress made a beeline straight for the wastelands. She guessed that only a crisis at the interdimensional vortex could have created the havoc she had seen back home.

She was correct.

Who could be behind this? she wondered, still not believing it could be a natural event. *Who has the power to pull this off?*

She mentally checked off a list of suspects who could possibly do the damage to the barrier and just as quickly dismissed each of them.

Cracks crisscrossed the energy barrier that separated the dimensions, one from another. If the vortex were to break free from the barrier, there would be nothing to hold back the various dimensions and keep them from spilling one on top of the other, mixing into a concoction unlike anything thousands of realities had ever seen.

Pure chaos.

The tendrils grew brighter, more intense until he had no choice but to shade her eyes lest an incandescence greater than the Sun permanently blind her.

She needed her eyes to face down her foe.

The barrier shattered.

Fragments of energy broke free and scattered to the four winds, creating havoc in their wake. Others floated untethered nearby. A few fell through the hole between the dimensions.

The vortex pushed free of its confines and set out across the wasteland, gobbling up everything in its path the way a tornado would have back on Earth.

The sorceress watched as the vortex moved away from her, off into the distance, leaving only devastation in its wake. She was about to take off in pursuit of it when she caught movement out of her peripheral vision.

I'm not alone!

The sorceress spun and came face to face with her enemy.

"You!?!"

"You seem surprised," the enemy said as a cunning smile flashed across her face.

"Why? Why are you doing this?" the sorceress asked.

The enemy's smile widened like a Cheshire grin.

"Because I can," she said simply.

The enemy gestured and the remnants of the barrier roared to life.

Another gesture and the pieces of the barrier the sorceress had journeyed to the wasteland to save bore down on her like magical missiles made of pure energy.

The sorceress tried to deflect them all, but the enemy was more powerful than she, more experienced, and more malevolent. She was evil incarnate, the woman she called the enemy, the polar opposite of the sorceress.

"Join me and I'll let you live," the enemy said,

her voice sweet and light, but tinged with malice. "There are still many more barriers to be broken. We could take them down together, you and I, until only one reality remains! Imagine it! Together, we can rule over all!"

"You're insane."

"I prefer to think of myself as a visionary," the enemy said, amused by her own humor.

"Go to hell!" the sorceress spat.

"You first."

The enemy's attack was violent, swift, and brutal.

Eldritch beams lanced out at the sorceress from all sides, striking far faster than her mystic shields could deflect them. Unable to withstand the onslaught, her shields cracked then shattered under the bombardment and the energy ribbons sliced through her body like a hot knife through Jell-O.

The sorceress screamed as a vortex of chaotic energy swirled around her, ripping away at her body and soul. The sound echoed across the cosmos, a melodic mixture of pain, rage, and failure.

Knowing her end was near, the sorceress made one final, desperate attempt to stop her enemy. There was only enough energy left for one last spell. *If I can't save my dimension, maybe I can save... maybe I can warn the next one.*

With her final thought, a spark of energy no larger than a marble leapt free from the sorceress and flew straight into the hole that separated this dimensional plane from its closest neighbors. Wherever it ended up, the sorceress hoped it could do some good.

And then she was gone, ripped apart by the vortex.

The enemy watched as the remaining energy that empowered the sorceress called Nightveil drifted away into the night, nothing but stardust.

The sorceress' lifeless body dropped out of the sky, igniting as it fell through the chaos storm before crashing into the graveyard that was the wasteland below.

The enemy smiled.

"One down…"

2.

Laura Wright was having an odd day.

Well, odd for her, anyway.

She awoke early, rested and ready to face the day. That in and of itself should have been her first clue that something was off. She couldn't remember the last time she had slept soundly through the night without being roused by some emergency or plagued by nightmares as her waking world bled into the realm of her dreams. After a long, hot, soapy shower, she slid into a pair of comfortable cotton shorts that were a size too small, but she loved them anyway. Then she pulled on a comfy old concert T-Shirt and slipped her toes into her favorite flip flops. After tying her hair up in a ponytail so she wouldn't have to comb it, Laura whipped up a nice breakfast of eggs with runny yokes and crunchy bacon with a side of toast and strawberry jam. An ice-cold glass of cranberry juice completed her idea of the perfect breakfast.

Food in hand, she headed out the front door.

She enjoyed her meal in silence on the front porch of her Victorian style home in the middle of the Florida Everglades. The home was her sanctuary, a gift from her mentor, Azagoth. More than just a home, it was the front-line defense between the Earth Laura called home and the incalculable number of dimensions that existed just a tick to the left or right of center. The house was magic itself and it hovered smoothly three feet above the alligator infested wetlands, safe from moss, mold, and trespassers.

For all the dangers kept under guard inside, Laura felt safe there.

She loved her home and couldn't imagine living anywhere else.

Sitting on the porch swing, legs swept up beneath her, she polished off her yummy breakfast and swayed back and forth on the spring breeze while catching up on some reading. She had been trying to finish the latest Barry Reese novel for weeks now, but every time she cracked it open, some emergency or another reared its ugly head and pulled her away.

Not so this day. She finished the remainder of the novel in a single sitting and wondered if the next book in the series was available yet. She would have to look it up on-line later and order it or teleport over to the local bookstore and see if they had it.

Stretched out on her porch swing, Laura stared out at the Everglades that surrounded her private sanctum and savored the beauty of nature. The house was old, older even than she was, though neither of them looked their actual age. The outside was in dire need of a paint job, which Laura could have easily accomplished with a few choice words and a wave of her nimble fingers, but she chose not to. The sanctum was her private escape from the chaos of the world at large. It had character and she

liked that about it, dry paint and all. It felt lived in--
--alive.

As protector of the Earth, Laura was prepared to leap into danger at a moment's notice, but fighting back the forces of evil, whether on her own as Nightveil or with her F.E.M.Force teammates, took a toll, both physically and mentally. When the mission ended, and the day had been saved, Laura always returned home to the sanctum to rest, revitalize, and replenish her power. That took care of the physical, but the mental was harder to reconcile.

Laura was exhausted.

Thankfully, it had been at least a week since any earth-shattering problem had required Nightveil's attention and she was enjoying every minute of the unexpected down time to counter the exhaustion. As Nightveil, she knew that lulls like this were usually the calm before the storm and that something was no doubt brewing that she would have to deal with eventually.

There was always something brewing.

However, it had been so long since she had been able to simply be Laura Wright, a normal person who reads books, washes dishes, and watches television that she planned to enjoy it as long as Azagoth allowed.

As Nightveil, Laura was known as the Mystic Maid of Might, the Mystic Mistress of the Nether Realms, Mistress Supreme of the Sorcerous Arts, and, on occasion, she was referred to simply as '*the super-hero with the weird starry cape.*' No matter where she appeared, Nightveil drew attention.

Laura Wright, on the other hand, could teleport into the city unseen and walk around the shopping district without anyone giving her a second glance.

They were two sides of the same coin, but the Nightveil side usually commanded the greater portion of her time, much to the detriment of Laura's personal life. She could scarcely recall the last time Laura had gone on a date or hit the town with friends of the non-superhuman variety, not that she had many of those these days. Protecting the multiverse from evil could be a lonely job at times.

After a couple of hours spent in quiet meditation while staring out into the relaxing beauty that was the Everglades, Laura stretched and yawned before meditation became a nap. A day off was one of those mysterious things she was always saying she wanted, but now that she had it, she found herself feeling out of sorts. She wasn't really quite sure what to do with herself.

Oh, let's face it, she was bored.

And a bored mystic, is a dangerous mystic, she heard Azagoth say in a memory from one of her early training sessions. Azagoth had been a stern taskmaster, but she had learned a great deal from the old mage.

Deciding on a change of scenery, Laura headed back inside, placed the finished novel on the bookshelf with care, and headed for her room. A quick change of clothes later, this time aided and abetted by her mystic powers, and Nightveil took to the skies, levitating above the Florida wetlands she called home. She loved the view from there, hovering above the trees and the water. It was peaceful, quiet, serene, and reminded her of the beauty this world had to offer. She hung motionless in the sky a moment, basking in the glorious sunshine. She didn't know where she was going, but...

That's when the perfect idea hit her.

A beach day. That's a great idea!

With a mischievous grin and a snap of her fingers, Nightveil vanished into a dimensional tunnel.

--only to reappear an instant later two hundred and sixty miles away.

"Daytona Beach," she muttered. "Perfect."

***

A day at the beach was indeed just what the sorcerer ordered.

Laura basked in the renewing warmth of the springtime sun, lying on the beach in her mystically created lounge chair, sunglasses propped leisurely atop her nose while a big, floppy hat shielded her face from sunburn. It was all unnecessary, of course. With her magics, she could have whipped up an incantation that would have allowed her to run around the beach stark naked all day and not turn so much as a hint of pink. The mystic energies that kept her safe from radiation when she crossed dimensional barriers also protected her from the Sun's harmful rays. Thanks to the magically created bikini she wore, Laura allowed herself to tan fully, but not burn. As a bonus, no tan lines.

Still, she wanted to blend in, not stand out.

Running around in her birthday suit, while liberating, would most certainly draw attention and attention was the last thing she was looking for on this trip. Peace, quiet, and tranquility were the order of the day.

Plus, she liked to look the part and what was more appropriate for the beach than a skimpy bikini? It felt good to be like everyone else there, just another beachcomber on the sand. Well, more or less. She doubted anyone else's bathing suit was conjured up by a magician's whim.

Daytona Beach was one of Florida's go-to getaway destinations. People came from all over the country to spend time on the sandy beaches. It was especially popular during Spring Break when teenagers and twenty-somethings came from all around to party. They also had a big stock car race there every year at the city's world-famous raceway.

Dealing with crowds was not usually Laura's idea of relaxing, but if you were looking for a place to get lost in the crowd, this was it. She whipped up a small perception filter that kept anyone from fully noticing her unless they were looking straight at her. That would keep everyone away so she could relax in relative peace and quiet, but also keep people from bumping into her or stepping over her while she tanned.

She had learned that lesson the hard way. It was on one of her first beach trips after developing her magical prowess. A big, burly drunk guy stepped on her because he couldn't see her. Granted, this was only slightly due to the perception filter though. As smashed as this guy had been, he probably wouldn't have seen her regardless. After stepping on her, she shouted the ubiquitous "Hey!" and that startled him. Off balance, he spilled his cup of beer and fresh hot dog with mustard and relish on her, which made her concentration waver.

As her concentration went, so too did the mystic bikini she had been projecting.

That's when everyone suddenly noticed her.

Laura couldn't get out of there fast enough. She had been embarrassed beyond belief, but she learned an important lesson about control and will power. It had been a long time since her concentration had been so easily broken.

Smiling at the memory that had once embarrassed her to the point of declaring that she would never set foot on a public beach again, Laura walked the beach, watching kids play in the sand while boys stared at the girls in bikinis. Even with the perception filter in place, she had even caught a few of those glances aimed her way and she blushed slightly at the attention. Though she had long since acclimated to the modern age of the twenty-first century she found herself living in, there was a part of Laura Wright that would always be a child of the 1920's. Some of those old practices were fully ingrained in her consciousness and hard to break.

Things were certainly more... reserved back then, she thought.

Of course, she had also found a lot of conveniences in the modern world. The Internet alone was a miraculous invention. The world seemed a much smaller place as people from all corners of the globe, an oxymoron, she knew, could freely communicate with one another on a daily basis virtually for free. She had often wondered what the world would have been like if the Internet had existed when she was a child. Could two World Wars have been averted if people from opposite sides of the planet had been able to talk with one another? Perhaps everyone's love of posting cat photos and humorous videos could have prevented much bloodshed and death.

Her favorite modern luxury was the microwave. She had been amazed by the power and speed with which food could be prepared in the home. It fascinated her. There were many nights she would stare as microwave popcorn popped in front of her. At the time, this too seemed like magic to her.

Lost in thought, Laura did not see the man running toward her until it was too late.

Nor did he see her until he slammed into her because he was looking off to the side instead of where he was running and with the perception filter in place, blocked her from view. It was a hard impact and it caught Laura completely off guard and knocked her off balance and derriere first into the surf. The cold water shocked her back to the moment as the big galoot fell on top of her with a grunt.

Laura steeled herself, ready for a fight, but her focus never wavered and the bathing suit projection remained in place.

Has some enemy found me?

She hated that her first thought was of attack. Living a life on constant struggle had made her more guarded, always on alert.

"I am so sorry!" the man said as he rolled off her, embarrassed as he tried too quickly to get to his feet in the shifting sand beneath them.

Predictably, he fell back into the water, this time landing on his bum in the wet sand.

Laura couldn't help but laugh at his predicament as she lay there resting on her elbows while shallow waves crested over her body.

On the second try, he managed to get to his feet. Once he was stable he held out a hand and, like a gentleman, offered to help Laura to her feet.

She accepted and let him pull her up out of the water until she was steady.

"Pete! Come on, man!" another voice called from far away.

Laura could see the man's friends nearby, each waving their hands wildly in the air.

He scooped up the frisbee that bobbed on the froth and with a mighty hurl, sent the disk flying across the sand toward his friends. Once caught, he waved them off and they continued playing without him.

"I am so sorry about that," he said.

"You said that already," Laura joked as she rang the salt water out her hair.

"I swear, I didn't even see you!"

"It's okay. It's just a little sand and water. No harm done."

"I'm Pete," he said, offering his hand and a goofy grin. "Pete Hall."

"Laura Wright." She shook his hand and offered him a smile in return.

"It was nice running into you, Laura Wright," he joked. "Literally."

"I'll bet," she said playfully. It had been too long since she had flirted with a stranger, especially one so much younger than her. It felt oddly liberating. Pete was probably twenty, maybe twenty-one and although she looked like she was in her twenties herself, Laura was painfully aware that there were quite a few decades separating them.

"Your friends are running off," she remarked, pointing at the group that was moving on down the beach throwing the frisbee around recklessly as they tripped over other pretty girls in bikinis on the beach.

"Or was I always your intended stop?"

She cocked her head to one side, sizing him up with a smirk and a raised eyebrow that would have made Mister Spock proud.

Busted, Pete blushed.

Laura smiled at his befuddlement.

"Well, not at first," Pete stammered. "I really didn't see you, but… but once I ran into you, I… well, you… that is, well, you can't blame a guy for trying, can you?"

"No. I guess I can't, Pete," she said with a playful laugh now that she decided to let him off the hook. "Now that I'm all wet and covered with sand, I might as well go for a swim."

She turned away from him and walked back into the surf.

Pete watched her walk away and his shoulders slumped with rejection. He was suddenly very interested in digging around in the wet sand with his toes.

"Pete?"

"Yes?" He looked up to see Laura standing knee deep in the salt water, looking back at him oddly.

"You coming or what?"

"What?"

Laura smiled. "Do. You. Want. To. Join. Me. For. A. Swim?" she said, punctuating each word to make sure he understood them.

"Uh, sure. Yeah," Pete stammered, surprised by the invitation, especially after figuring he had blown it big time. A pretty girl like Laura was way out of his league so he wasn't about to argue with her. A wide toothy grin firmly in place, Pete ran into the surf after her, splashing water in his wake.

A minute later, they were both in the water, swimming side by side out of the shallows and headed toward deeper depths. Eventually, they stopped and, while treading water, got to know each other better.

"We should have brought surfboards," Pete said.

"Nah. Nothing but baby waves here," Laura told him. "If you want some real surfing, you have to head down the coast a bit. That's where you'll find the *righteous curls*."

"I'm game if you are," he said, trying to be smooth and failing.

Laura smiled at him, somehow managing to keep from chuckling at his awkwardness. She appreciated that he was making an effort and actually found it somewhat endearing, maybe even cute, but Pete really was trying too hard. He needed to relax. She started to tell him as much when out of the corner of her eye she caught movement, something out of place.

Something that was not supposed to be there.

The glowing object entered the atmosphere and fell straight toward them.

Oh, crap! Now what?

3.

"We should head back in," Laura Wright said.

"So soon?" Pete Hall said sadly.

"Sorry, but something's come up and I really need to go."

"What could possibly have come up out here? Can't you just swim with me for a little while?"

"Maybe some other time," she said regretfully, nudging him to start heading toward shore. "This is the end of my vacation and I have to go to work."

"What kind of work do you do?" he asked, trying to keep the conversation moving forward.

"I'm... well, it's hard to describe, but I'm part of an emergency management response team." She pointed at the darkening sky. "See that? That's trouble. We're going to have to close the beaches and get everyone out of the water before that storm hits."

"Oh, I'm sorry to hear that." It was impossible for Pete to hide the crushing disappointment in his big puppy dog eyes.

"Me too," Laura said. "Let's head in, okay?"

"Okay." Pete was clearly confused since they had just gotten out to the deep. It seemed a little fast to be heading back in, but he decided not to question it. Either she was telling the truth about the storm or was using a few dark clouds as an excuse to get away from him, not that he thought he had done anything to scare her off.

"Maybe we can grab a bite to eat before you leave," he suggested. "There's this great little restaurant on the boardwalk that serves up a mean loaded tater tot bowl. It's delicious."

"Maybe," she said. "If there's time."

The possibility of their impromptu date continuing spurred Pete and he started paddling. Sadly, she suspected there would not be time for them to grab a bite. Not today. They swam toward shore with Laura moving faster than her companion this time around.

Once she reached the beach, she turned to look for the flicker of errant energy she had glimpsed. It stood out like a neon sign against the darkening clouds. Thunder echoed in the distance.

There!

It burned bright across the cloudy sky, trailed by green, sparkling flames as it fell toward earth like a meteor. Unlike so many others before it that had fallen through the atmosphere, this one was not burning up on entry.

In fact, it looked like it was growing brighter.

And then it changed direction.

So much for a beach day, Laura thought.

Pete had just reached the beach when the flaming object hit the water behind him. It exploded silently on impact, sending waves of green light and energy out in all directions. He was walking toward the sand in waist deep water when a wave shot out from the point of impact and caught Pete unawares. The wave knocked him off his feet and dragged him beneath the salty water before he had a chance to scream or take a deep breath.

There was no time for Laura to warn him, let alone use her powers to forcibly move him out of harm's way in time.

All she could do was watch as both Pete and the flaming meteor disappeared beneath the waves.

And then they were gone.

***

The sea settled quickly.

On the beach, Laura waited for her new friend to resurface, worried about what had happened to him. With a thought, her bikini morphed into her work clothes. Gone was the young woman enjoying a day at the beach. In her place stood Nightveil: Mystic Maid of Might with her star-filled cape fluttering freely in the breeze.

Based on her experiences, Nightveil suspected that whatever had hit the water was not going to simply sink to the bottom and stay there.

She was right.

The creature erupted from the water with a roaring inhuman howl.

Though it held the outward appearance of a man: two arms, one head, hands, and the like, the creature's features were encased in a mass of swirling water that resembled a walking water spout. Whatever the thing was originally, Nightveil knew it was not a product of Earth's ocean from the glowing green tint the vortex of water held.

The creature threw its arms wide as if ripping away a shirt or a chain around its chest. Water flew off of his arms like tiny missiles, hitting with far more force than that of a water balloon.

The energy source that hit the water was most definitely not of human shape in its native form. The only reason it looked human now, Nightveil deduced, was because it had merged with a human host. She had a sneaking suspicion she knew that host personally.

"Pete?" Nightveil asked. "Are you in there?"

With an inhuman roar, the vortex reached out an arm toward her and clumsily blasted a stream of water charged with crackling bursts of energy in her direction.

Nightveil sidestepped the first attack easily. It was an attack fueled by instinct more than anger. There appeared to be little thought behind it, but that did not diminish its power. The impact punched a three-foot deep hole in the beach and sent sand flying in all directions.

If that had hit someone... Nightveil thought.

Someone screamed and the crowd reacted, throwing the beach into chaos as the assembled crowd of beachcombers ran in all directions. In their haste to reach safety, some were knocked down and trampled.

Nightveil wanted to help, but there was no time to evacuate the beach and hold off the creature. She would have to keep it occupied while the others ran to safety.

The creature roared and attacked again, its attention focused on the caped hero.

Nightveil moved like lightning, zigging and zagging across the suddenly dark summer sky, deftly avoiding the charged bolts the elemental warrior tossed at her as she led the vortex water creature out to sea and away from the beach and the innocent civilians scattered about the sand. Most were fleeing to safety, but several had stopped to grab their phones and film the battle.

Her flight was choreographed poetry, pirouetting around attacks while throwing off counterattacks of her own while leading it away from land and the spectators who remained.

The elemental was formidable, a powerhouse of pure energy tapped into nature's fury. The surging strength of the ocean waves only added to its brute Force, which was already considerable. Where Nightveil fought with Grace and skill, her enemy subsisted on rage and instinct.

That would prove the creature's ultimate weakness, but first she would have to burn off its excess energy and free Pete from its clutches.

Thankfully, she remembered the lessons of her youth.

Water boiled away into a harmless gas. Some science had changed since her early years, but there were some immutable truths. All she needed was a moment to catch her breath and craft an appropriate spell to boil away the water feeding the vortex. The first step was breaking contact between the vortex and the sea below. The Atlantic Ocean was vast and could potentially feed the creature indefinitely. She needed to sever that connection.

Not that her enemy planned to cooperate, if the swirling arm of water that shot toward her like a hurricane was any indication.

She tried to dodge it, to duck beneath the turbulent vortex, but wasn't fast enough and Nightveil was tossed into the swirling maw of the storm where she was tossed back and forth like a rag doll in the grip of an angry attack dog. Nightveil found herself flailing end over end inside the vortex until she couldn't tell up from down, right from left. Her cape pulled her in one direction while her legs went another.

I'm going to be ripped apart if I can't get out of this fast, she thought.

"By the eye of Azagoth, I command you!" she started.

Before she could utter another syllable, a wall if water slammed into her and sent her flying head over heels deeper into the vortex.

I'm getting creamed in here!

And suddenly she was surrounded by an ocean of calm.

"The hell?"

All around her, the storm raged, but she had been pulled into the middle of the tempest. The air immediately dropped from hurricane gale force to a light, summer breeze. Even the humidity lowered as she hovered in the calmness that could only be found at the center of any storm.

"The eye!" she shouted. "Azagoth be praised! I'm in the beast's eye!"

It didn't take long for the creature to figure out what had happened and where she had gone.

The swirling walls of water began closing in on her.

Okay. So, it's clearly not stupid.

The eye was shrinking fast.

In a moment, she would once again be totally submerged.

Luckily, all she needed was a moment.

Acting quickly, Nightveil spoke an enchantment that sent a bubble of raw force expanding away from her in all directions as it grew larger and larger until--

--the giant swirling beast exploded outward like a burst water balloon.

No longer held aloft by the tempest's winds, Nightveil felt the world fall out from beneath her as gravity reasserted its pull and she splashed harmlessly into the waiting waves of the Atlantic.

Pete, the beast's unwitting host, dropped face first into the surf nearby. He wasn't moving.

She swam over to him and, once she was certain he was alive and undamaged, Nightveil scooped Pete up with a bit of magic and gently spirited him to dry land. He would recover, but she feared the nightmares that would no doubt haunt his dreams for weeks to come.

There was nothing she could do about that now. She would make sure to check in on Pete later to make sure he fully recovered or help him battle his nightmares if need be, but at the moment there were far more pressing matters that needed to be dealt with. Pete would have to be okay on his own for a while as she took care of business.

At her feet, a tiny green vortex spun, barely powerful enough to reach her ankles. She couldn't help but smile at how cute it looked now that it wasn't threatening to destroy the beach and everyone on it.

"Aren't you precious?" she said in that tone reserved for playful pets and newborn babies. "Now, what shall we do with you, huh?"

With a wave of her fingers, a small purple orb formed around the vortex and lifted it into the air where it spun harmless before her.

"Are you responsible for this storm?" Nightveil asked, her voice barely a whisper. "I wonder where you came from? Such power as yours did not originate on this plane." She looked skyward at something only she could see.

"Come on, little vortex," Nightveil said as she floated heavenward. "Let's check on Pete then see if we can't get you back home."

When her feet touched the sand again, Pete was sitting up, coughing the water from his lungs. A few bystanders were helping him. He was physically okay, but he looked out of it to Nightveil. Fearing that seeing her in full costume might spike his anxiety, she mystically morphed it back into the bikini he saw her wearing.

Pete coughed and spit up water. He hurt all over, but wasn't sure why. The last thing he remembered was swimming with…

"Laura?" Pete called, looking around for her.

When he couldn't find her, he feared the worst. He tried to get to his feet to search for her, but the dizziness made standing difficult. She might have been hurt. Or worse. His intentions were good, but the battle had taken more out of Pete Hall than he knew.

"Pete!"

"Oh, Laura. Thank goodness. I was so worried about you."

"I'm fine, Pete. Are you okay?" Laura asked, crouching next to him.

"I... I think so," he stammered. "What was that?"

"I think lightning hit the water," Laura said. It sounded as plausible as his being possessed by an energy vortex creature from another plane of existence.

"Am I okay?" he asked. "Was I electrocuted?"

Laura chuckled slightly. "You were just getting out of the water when it struck. I don't think there's anything to worry about, but have someone take you to the hospital and get checked out just in case."

"Can't you take me?"

"I still have work to do, but I promise to check on you later," she said. "Besides, here come your buddies and they look real worried about you."

"Oh, I'm going to catch such a ribbing for this," Pete said.

"Nah," Laura said before planting a kiss on his, which only added to his stunned demeanor. "That'll give them something else to focus on."

Pete fell backward into the sand, a big smile on his face.

Laura vanished into the crowd as Pete's friends arrived.

Once they were high enough, Laura's Nightveil costume reappeared. She took one last look at the beach as Pete was being helped to a van by his buddies. At least he was safe now. She had to return he vortex to where it belonged and she had a good idea where to start looking for the right match to its dimensional amplitude.

Leaving Pete Hall and a beach full of confused vacationers wondering what the heck had just happened, Nightveil and the vortex flew into the darkening sky--

--and vanished in a burst of light.

4.

At the edge of infinity, chaos reigned.

Explosions of colors bloomed in a miasma of intricate patterns all around Nightveil the moment she breached the dimensional barrier that separated her realm from the wasteland at the center of the multiverse. The colors were more vibrant than she had ever seen naturally occur in nature or created by man.

Normally, she found it all quite beautiful, spectacular even.

This time, it was nauseating and blindingly bright.

She wretched and the breakfast she had so richly enjoyed splattered across the cracked desert floor below. Starbursts of color blossomed all around her. It was quite disorienting until her senses adjusted to it. Her head pounded in rhythm with the bursts until her eyes threatened to pop out of their sockets and seek refuge someplace less severe.

Nightveil had first visited the wasteland roughly a decade or so earlier in the company of her mentor, the wizard Azagoth. Even then she had been in awe of the blossoming colors that surrounded her. It was sensory overload and she was so glad that Azagoth was there to help her get through it. He taught her how to focus, to block it out. He referred to it as mental sensory deprivation and it worked. This was during her training years and the wasteland made her feel small and insignificant in the grand scheme of things. She often suspected it was exactly that feeling that her mentor had hoped to elicit from her.

If so, he succeeded.

She felt small and alone.

Helpless.

Like an ant on the highway.

The wasteland reminded her of a desert, big and empty, the ground parched and cracked as if from too much heat and too little water. Only here, at the center of everything, it was not the absence of moisture that threatened to swallow up anything that lived-- it was magic.

Azagoth told her that the Crossroads of Infinity was where magic began and ended. The vortex doled out what it felt each dimensional realm needed to sustain it. Some received more than others, but each dimension was awarded a protector, someone who would watch over that dimension and keep it safe.

Then he told her that she was destined to be that protector.

"Bullshit," she said at the time.

She did not believe him.

Even now, she wasn't sure she truly believed she had been chosen for such an exalted position in the grand scheme of things. She knew what she did as Nightveil saved lives and helped people, but that was a far cry from saving the multiverse.

She told him as much, but Azagoth shrugged it off, or at least he would have shrugged it off if he had shoulders, and launched into a parable about a young boy who had a sacred responsibility thrust upon his tiny shoulders. She didn't know how the story ended because she tuned her mentor out shortly into the tale, distracted by the terrifying beauty erupting all around her.

When he got back around to the wasteland, Azagoth told her that the magical energies that created the multiverse also seeded it, nurtured each and every one of the countless dimensions that all intersected in the center of the wasteland. As the energies left the wasteland and entered their dimension of choice, the wasteland fell further and further into decay and ruin. She often wondered if there was only a finite amount of mystical energy to go around. If so, could the magic conceivably run out?

It was all speculative, of course. Azagoth taught her that the wasteland looked like a desert to her because that was something that Laura Wright's subconscious mind understood. Azagoth described the wasteland as looking different for every poor soul who dared glance upon it. The one thing all agreed on was that the wasteland was aptly named as everyone saw some kind of lifeless landscape of some kind.

"Even a mind as powerful as yours cannot fully comprehend the power of the Crossroads of Infinity," Azagoth had told her during her training.

She took the wizard at his word, but when she asked her mentor what he saw when he looked upon the wasteland with his big, powerful eye, he responded with silence.

The Wasteland still resembled a desert to her, even though she was no longer the same novice young mystic she had been on her initial visit. Dry, parched, and cracked, it stretched out to infinitesimal distance until it was swallowed by the vortex on the horizon. Now, Laura believed that the non-comforting wasteland was unwelcoming on purpose. There was no need for anyone to spend much time in this place. An inhospitable wasteland would turn away those wishing to set up a permanent residence.

As devoid of life as the wasteland was, the sky above the desert floor was another matter entirely. In sheer opposition to the lifelessness below, the sky was filled with wonder. Colors from all ends of the spectrum bloomed into existence, falling over and melding together before the next explosion of color replaced it. It reminded Laura of a mixture of a hundred water colors when color was dropped onto a wet canvas and fireworks exploding in the night sky.

It was beautiful and she could stare at the hypnotic colors for hours on end.

But this was no time for sightseeing. She had come to the Crossroads of Infinity for a purpose. Her traveling companion was eager to return to the vortex it called home.

The tiny tornado jerked and juked inside her force bubble, trying to break free to rejoin the vortex. Even at this distance, the pull was incredible. Although returning it to the place from which it sprang was why she had journeyed there, she also wanted to make sure that it truly belonged there. There were more than a couple of moments in history where things appeared one way only to later be revealed to be another.

Not a mistake she was prone to repeat.

Nightveil planned to be absolutely certain her new winsome friend truly belonged before returning the errant elemental back from whence it came.

"Let's find a place for you while I look around," Nightveil told the tiny tornado.

She opened a fold in her cape and placed the elemental into a pocket dimension created for her private use. The vortex would be safe, but more importantly, it would not be able to do any damage in there.

The tiny tornado roared its displeasure, but at its diminutive size, she found the elemental's indignation more cute than fearful.

With her charge safely tucked away, Nightveil floated high above the wasteland. She could have walked the distance, but she found contact with the ground here most unsettling. It was as though a tingling electrical shock hit her foot with each step that filled her with dread. She couldn't help but wonder if solid ground was what the desert actually was or not. She hoped it was not some malevolent force that she could not recognize for what it truly was so she tried to avoid contact as much as possible. She had once had a dream that the wasteland was alive. It turned to quicksand beneath her feet and swallowed her whole, a tasty morsel for the cosmic creature that pretended to be a desert. That was the last time she made actual contact with the wasteland.

Besides, it was a long walk to the vortex and flying was faster.

An hour into her journey, she saw something that looked out of place.

What is that? she wondered.

Her previous visits had not shown any indigenous creatures living on the wasteland, but there was something laying on the path ahead.

Remember, the wasteland is fraught with dangers, Azagoth's warning echoed in her memory. *Take nothing at face value*, her mentor had warned on a previous visit.

It remained good advice.

Curious, but also cautious, Nightveil landed near whatever it was that littered the path. It took careful concentration, but she kept an inch of air between the bottom of her shoes and the surface.

"Hello?" she said. She hadn't expected an answer from the dark, charred thing and she was not disappointed. The wasteland road was still, not even a hot desert breeze mussed her hair.

She crouched in front of the cracked figure and felt the electricity tingle beneath her feet. Even though she wasn't in direct contact, she felt the tingling sensation from close proximity. She reached out to the thing, already knowing what she would find.

It was a body.

Dead.

She looked around instinctively. On Earth, a dead body on the highway brought vultures out to feast on the carrion. She half expected to find cosmic versions of those vile beasts along the wasteland and was surprised when she did not see anything resembling them nearby.

"I wonder who you were?" she whispered before looking up at the long stretch of black, charred corpses that littered the path. "Who all of you were?"

Something terrible had happened there. The corpses confirmed that. What she did not know was who could have done such a thing and why. Sure, she had her share of enemies who wouldn't think twice about killing innocents who dared brave a pilgrimage to the wasteland, but there was no reason for such wanton murder.

Not that she hadn't run across fiends who murdered for fun in the past either.

After all this time, such brutality still surprised her.

Deciding that there was nothing that could be done for the corpses, Nightveil took to the sky once more, happy to put distance between herself and the cracked highway. This time she moved with more alacrity toward her destination. Something was wrong. She could feel it.

As she approached, Nightveil could see that there were already two others standing before the vortex.

No. That was wrong.

They weren't standing.

They were fighting.

The combatants were both mystics, furiously tossing energy blasts at one another, but they were also brawlers, occasionally grappling hand to hand before pulling away for another magical attack. As

Nightveil drew closer, she saw one of the robed fighters slug the other one with a left hook that would have made Ms. Victory proud.

The first punch sent her reeling.

The second punch knocked the fighter out of the sky and sent her plummeting toward the desert floor below. The impact sent dust and dirt flying into the air as the fighter crashed into the hard-packed ground.

Staggered, the fighter pushed herself up from the newly formed crater, bruised and battered, but still in the fight. With the back of her hand, she wiped away blood from her busted lip.

Nightveil marveled at her strength, her will power. The woman crawled free of the crater and turned so that Nightveil could clearly see her face. She immediately recognized her. Until that moment, she wasn't sure which side to choose in this fight, but when she recognized the combatant it all clicked into place.

Alizarin Crimson.

Nightveil knew her well. Alizarin Crimson was one of her toughest foes and had come close to killing her on more than one occasion. There were worse things than death though, and Nightveil had encountered a few of them at the hands of this woman. Kidnapped, tortured, enslaved, forced to hurt others in that witch's name. These were the memories that bubbled angrily to the surface when Nightveil saw Alizarin Crimson.

Alizarin Crimson was not a nice person.

Nightveil shouted her hated foe's name as she adjusted course to intercept without hesitation. She hadn't come to the wasteland looking for a fight, but wherever Alizarin Crimson went, death and destruction surely followed. It was Nightveil's sacred duty to stop evil wherever it reared its ugly head and she was very good at her job.

With their history together, there was no denying that Alizarin Crimson was evil incarnate.

Distracted by Nightveil's angry shout, Alizarin Crimson was not prepared for the opposition from the rear. She spun at the sound, turning her back on one enemy as another attacked.

Flying fast, Nightveil slammed hard into Alizarin Crimson and sent her flying. Knocked off her feet, she fell back into the crater she had dug herself out of only moments earlier.

Nightveil alighted at the crater's edge, her anger overriding the tingling in her toes from contact with the cracked desert surface. Tendrils of pent up energy crackled around her gloved fists, waiting to be released. In their last encounter, Alizarin Crimson was presumed killed. Nightveil had never expected the opportunity for a rematch would ever come around again.

Now that it had, she wasn't going to let the opportunity pass by unanswered.

"Stay down!" Nightveil warned. "Whatever scheme you're planning, Alizarin Crimson, you won't get away with it this time! Not again!"

Alizarin Crimson looked up at her new attacker. At first, she seemed surprised to find Nightveil standing over her, energy crackling around her balled fists, angry and ready for a fight. That was not the Nightveil she remembered.

"You?" Alizarin Crimson said, confused. She looked around, probably trying to find her foe, the one who knocked her down initially. "How are you…"

Nightveil was curious where the robed warrior had gotten to herself, but she knew better than to divert her attention away from a foe as cagey as this one. Whoever she had been fighting, Alizarin Crimson looked scared. It was not a feeling she usually ascribed to the evil sorceress. Could it be that the great Alizarin Crimson had finally picked on an opponent who would not show her compassion?

"You were maybe expecting someone else?" Nightveil asked.

"I think that would be me," a new voice answered. It was a husky voice, like someone out of an old noir movie whose primary diet subsisted of whiskey and cigarettes, but with a hint of sultry smoothness.

It also sounded somewhat familiar.

Nightveil looked up as the robed figure hovered above, the cape of her cloak fluttering in the non-existent wind.

It was a familiar cape.

A cape filled with stars.

Now it was Nightveil's turn to be confused.

The robed mystic lowered herself to the desert floor, stopping to hover only half of an inch above the dry, cracked dirt as Nightveil had done earlier. Like her cloak, the newcomer's outfit was also familiar. The one-piece skintight sleeveless jumpsuit was dark blue, much darker than she had seen it before. The legs and thighs sported small cutout windows that showed tanned flesh beneath. A blue mask covered her piercing blue eyes. Deep purple boots, belt, and cloak with hood rounded out the ensemble. The inside of the cloak was a field of twinkling stars and spirals of other dimensions alive with wonder. It was almost identical to Nightveil's own, with just a few minor variations.

"Run," Alizarin Crimson warned before the enemy blasted her into unconsciousness.

But Nightveil wasn't listening. She stared at the newcomer, the woman who had beaten Alizarin Crimson before and was apparently there to finish the job.

"It's... you," Nightveil said, her throat suddenly parched. "How is..."

"How is this possible?" the newcomer asked, smiling as she spoke. "It's simple, really. Here at the Crossroads of Infinity, all things are possible, are they not? Surely, your mentor taught you that much."

"I... I guess so..." Nightveil stammered. Try as she might, she could not find the words to express what it felt like to come face to face with another version of herself, though one a few years older and weathered. A few extra wrinkles around the eyes and mouth, a couple of strands of silver in her hair, but otherwise identical. Sure, she understood it was possible. With all the myriad dimensions in existence, there were likely to be an equal number of Laura Wrights and Nightveils out there. She had simply never expected to encounter one. Especially not at the center of the multiverse.

"Laura Wright, I presume," the newcomer said.

Nightveil nodded. "Uh, huh."

"Thank you for helping me apprehend Alizarin Crimson, Laura."

"Happy to help," Nightveil said, finding her voice. "I take it you both are from a neighboring dimension?"

"Something like that," the smiling Nightveil said.

Nightveil looked down at her fallen foe and shook her head. "What was she up to this time? No good, I bet."

The smiling Nightveil snorted a laugh as she looked down at her beaten enemy lying at her feet. "Actually, if you can believe it, she was trying to save the multiverse," she said with a throaty giggle. "She was trying to be the good guy."

That caught the mystic maid off guard. "I'll bet. She's... Wait? What did you say? Who was she trying to save it from?"

The smiling Nightveil turned back to look at her other self.

"From me," she said.

That was the last thing Nightveil heard before her dimensional doppelganger punched her square in the face.

After that there was only darkness.

--and the sensation of falling.

5.

At the edge of infinity, chaos reigned.

And the architect of that chaos was loving every minute of it.

The enemy looked out over the carnage she had wrought and smiled at the beauty of it all. Even in its death throes, the Crossroads of Infinity was awash in vibrant colors and rapturous energy discharges that lit up the sky above the wasteland like it was the Fourth of July.

Below the cosmic fireworks, the wasteland was littered with the burnt corpses of those who dared to oppose her. They were alike, more or less. Heroic. Superior. Eager to fly into danger without a moment's thought to her own safety. With only a handful of exceptions, each one was a doppelganger of the other. They were all born in different dimensions from one another, separated by an invisible barrier between realities, but the majority of them all had one thing in common.

They were born as Laura Wright.

Some had kept the name while others had changed it. Some fought crime with only a couple of .45's, a distracting skimpy costume, and high heels. Others clad themselves in the cloak of magic, having become a powerful sorceress under the teachings of one of the elder gods, most notably, a peculiar entity that looked like a fuzzy brick with a giant eye in its center known as Azagoth.

She had killed her fair share of Azagoth doppelgangers as well. Mostly out of spite for training her deadliest enemies and being a general nuisance.

Most of the Laura Wright's she encountered had taken up the mantle of Nightveil, protector of the weak and helpless in most dimensions, savior of the world in others. Still other versions of her wore skimpy costumes and danced on poles for cash. The dimensional shift was a wonder. All it took was one slight change to create a divergent reality, a new dimension where life continued on a new path.

The enemy believed that there was only a finite amount of mystic energy to go around. With each new alternate reality, she was certain that the main source of the power, the vortex at the center of the Crossroads of Infinity was being diminished, spread out amongst the various dimensions to the various versions of Laura Wright.

She wanted that power for herself.

For that, each and every version of Laura Wright had to die.

Laura Wright was an odd puzzle. On the face of it, she was a soft-spoken, good girl from a simpler time, almost puritanical in her beliefs, yet her choice of costumed garb revealed a more risqué side of her. It was that side that the enemy wanted to harness.

She had beaten each and every one of them as they stood against her. Oh, all of the encounters started out more or less the same way. Laura Wright would make her way to the Crossroads of Infinity to stand against the enemy waiting for her. Most went by the moniker of Nightveil, but some surprised her. There were others called the Blue Bulleteer, the Silver Moray, The Maiden of Might, and a couple of Laura Wrights who were adventurers without a costumed super-hero identity who relied upon their skills and wits instead of mystical powers.

Not that it mattered.

They all fell before her.

As would the next to arrive and the one after that.

She smiled as she stared across the wasteland at her handy work. Each of the newly rotting corpses had been lured to the Crossroads of Infinity as part of an orchestrated plot to take out those who could possibly stand against the enemy and her plans. There were only a couple of names on the list, but each divergent dimension was home to another copy of the same troublemaker who might stand in her way. They only way to ensure success was to eliminate them all so she set a trap.

The trap was a sophisticated one, but also deceptively simple. She knew her enemy as intimately as she knew herself and that gave her an edge. Her adversaries had a fatal flaw that she could exploit. Almost every version of Laura Wright was a good and honest person with a natural desire to help those in trouble. While most might find these traits admirable, the enemy understood the truth.

It made her predictable.

And that was why the enemy would win.

Before the final barrier came down, she would

wipe out each and every Nightveil or version of Laura Wright she could find until there were none to stand against her.

On that day, her victory would be assured.

"It's beautiful, is it not?" she said without turning to the person who walked up behind her. The enemy's partner was as silent as a mouse, but even she knew better than to think of herself as the enemy's better. The woman was evil incarnate and her power knew no bounds.

Nor did her thirst for vengeance.

"I love what you've done with the place," the partner said.

"Try to contain your enthusiasm, my dear," the enemy said. She was still not looking at the new arrival. "Everything moves according to plan."

"And the magician?"

"She will come to me in time," the enemy said. "They all fall before me in time."

"Careful, now," her friend said. "Overconfidence could cost your dearly."

"Watch yourself, witch!" the enemy said, finally turning to stare face to face at her companion. Tendrils of orange energy spiked angrily around her hands. "You and I go back a long way, but never presume that means you are my equal."

"I would never presume such," her companion said, her eyes watching the energy dance and grow around her friend's fingers. "You have made your position plain multiple times. I know where I stand and I will always have your back."

"And that is why you are here with me instead of down there with… them."

"There must be thousands of them down there," the companion said, floating above the corpse-strewn wasteland. "Are there many dimensions left to cleanse before we're ready to take down the barrier?"

The enemy laughed. It was a sound that gripped at her companion's heart and squeezed.

"I feel like I missed a joke," she said, afraid that she had said the wrong thing. The last thing she wanted to do was incur her wrath and end up one of the charred corpses she floated above.

"There are millions of divergent realities still to be cleansed," the enemy said. "And more spring into existence daily."

"Sounds like a never-ending chore to eradicate them all."

"I can be patient," the enemy said softly. "I have waited this long, I can endure more. I'm playing a long game, my friend. I knew it wouldn't be quick nor would it be easy, but when I'm done... oh, when the last domino falls... it will be glorious."

"And Nightveil? The last one got away."

"A bit of luck," she said. "With the dimensional barriers weakening, it was little more than dumb luck that she fell into a crack in the barrier. Who knows what is likely to await her on the other side of that doorway?"

"I was taught never to believe in luck. Actually, I believe you're the one who taught me that lesson, if I recall correctly."

The enemy groaned.

"Don't test me," she warned.

"I wouldn't dream of it."

"The sorceress is nothing to me now. With the powers from those I've already cleansed added to my own not inconsiderable powers, I am ready to face down an army of Nightveils. She may have escaped, but she was beaten. When she returns…"

"What makes you think she'll ever come back here?" the companion asked.

"Perhaps you are unfamiliar with the stubborn streak associated with her kind. They call themselves super-heroes. Such arrogance. Trust me. She will be back and when she returns, I will destroy her as I have done to all who came before her."

"You really think you can beat them all?"

"I know I can," the enemy said with confidence. "They will all fell before me, my friend. Just as this one fell, so too shall the next to arrive and the one after that and the one after that until they are all gone and only one Laura Wright remains."

She smiled, enjoying the dramatic pause.

"Me."

"Only you?"

"Yes," the enemy said. "Like them, I am also named Laura Wright. I, however, am the original article, as it were. I was born in the original universe and I was the first to bear the name Laura Wright. All of the others, the alternate dimensions and divergent realities all sprang from my original dimension. From there, each decision, each ripple in time branched out until there were countless others. Don't you see? Splitting off new realities from mine has diluted the purity of my magic. My power has been splintered and re-splintered millions upon millions of times until the power was on the verge of extinction!"

"How would it…"

"You don't understand," the enemy interrupted. "But I can feel the power being leeched away and given to inferior copies of the original. I had to act before it was too late."

"What have you done?" her companion asked.

"I am setting right what once went wrong," the enemy said. "With each copy I destroy, the power returns to me. I am stronger than I have been in years! Can you not see it? The universe is in chaos. It was never meant to diverge into a multiverse. That was a cosmic mistake. One that I aim to correct. I will save the universe. My universe."

Laura Wright stood at the edge of infinity and admired the chaos she had set into motion and laughed at the beauty of it all.

"Soon, the power will be mine," she said, voice rising above the chaos winds. "Mine and mine alone, as it was always meant to be. On that day, when the ultimate mystic potential is under my control, only then will I become the most powerful woman in the universe."

She barked a laugh that terrified her companion.

"Then, I will hold the power to shape reality in whatever way I see fit. On that day, a new golden age of humanity will begin. And I… Laura Wright… Nightveil… will be their queen. Mark my words."

She laughed again and the chaos erupted in time. "On that day, all will be right with the world again."

6.

Nightveil floated on a sea of stars.

She knew it was all a dream, that her flesh and blood body was lying unconscious on the desert wasteland that ringer the Crossroads of Infinity. Unless her doppelganger from another dimension had moved her, which was entirely possible.

The stars danced about her like little pixies with tiny wings that left a trail of glittery stardust in their wake. They danced in tune to a melody only they could hear.

Back when she was a mystic in training, the wizard Azagoth first introduced her to astral projection. With concentration and practice, Azagoth taught her that a mystic could separate their living consciousness from their flesh and blood body for a limited time without either entity suffering any ill effects.

Her first attempts only lasted minutes a piece, but eventually, Laura learned how to release her astral form for hours at a time. Once, she managed to go a full day, but dared not deprive her body of the essentials of life for that length of time again unless it was necessary.

As with most otherworldly magicks, time moved differently inside the astral plane. There was no real constant, only what the astral traveler brought with her. Before she learned how to slow down and appreciate her surroundings, time had moved quite quickly for Laura Wright. Now that she had learned to, how had her teacher put it again? Ah, yes, he told her to "*stop and smell the roses sometimes*" and he had been correct.

The past few hours were still a jumble in her mind. The other Nightveil, the one who had knocked her lights out, was it possible that she was the villain and Alizarin Crimson was the hero? It was a difficult concept to grasp.

Perhaps they were from a mirror dimension like on that old episode of Star Trek where the good guys were evil and the bad guys were the heroes. Thankfully, her evil twin hadn't sported facial hair.

She laughed at her own joke, but wondered how she was going to get out of her current predicament. Laura guessed that only a few minutes had passed since she had been rendered unconscious in the real world so she had time to think.

Unless her evil counterpart was planning to kill her flesh and blood body.

Time to wake up, Laura, Nightveil told herself.

Nothing happened.

Okay, that's not good. Let's try that again.

Still nothing.

WAKE UP!!!

Laura's eyes snapped open.

She was back in her own body again.

And she could move.

She looked up and saw a giant city rushing toward her.

Immediately, Nightveil knew two things.

One, she was no longer in the wasteland and two…

Two was a doozy.

Two, she realized that she wasn't floating on a sea of stars. Instead, she was falling to her death over an unknown city.

And the ground was fast approaching.

***

Laura Wright watched the meteor streak across the evening sky.

Fire trailed behind as it fell through the atmosphere, cutting a flaming swath across the dusk-colored sky. Even from her vantage atop a thirty-two story building, Laura knew it would not completely burn up before it hit one of the balloons that hovered above the city's skyscrapers.

And she was right.

The unidentified falling object, which she was no longer convinced was a meteor, slammed into one of the many dirigibles hovering high above the city.

The helium erupted into a blazing fireball on impact, blossoming in an explosion that would have been awe-inspiring if it hadn't taken out one of their protection balloons.

Both the balloon and the object dropped out of the sky together, pulled down by the tether that locked the balloon's position in place.

They crashed in an alley near her position.

Laura was on the move before the balloon hit the ground, leaping from rooftop to rooftop like a jungle cat stalking its prey from the treetops, her red cape flapping in the breeze behind her. The city was ever-changing in its layout, but at the moment, she knew it backward and forward, which was important in her line of work. She had studied the buildings and fire escapes until she could travel from one end of the city to the other blindfolded if she had to.

That knowledge helped her reach the crash site before even the fire brigade, the police, or the military.

The balloon's thick canvas hide was more or less intact, only ruptured at the seams with singe marks from the fire that thankfully burned hot and fast then extinguished itself just as quickly. There was only smoke now that it was on the ground. Laura wondered if it might be salvageable. If they could repurpose it and get it back in the air in time, they could plug the newly formed gap in their security net. All she needed was…

The balloon coughed.

In the blink of an eye, Laura held her trusted .45, having deftly plucked it from the holster on her hip. The safety was off, hammer cocked, and ready for action. She kept it trained on the balloon.

"You! Under there! Step out slowly!"

The bag moved as the person trapped beneath it slowly wriggled out from beneath the heavy canvas. "Don't shoot," a feminine voice called.

"You do as you're told and I think we can avoid that," Laura said.

"Sounds good to me," the purple robed figure said as she clawed free of the heavy canvas tomb.

"I'm called Nightveil. And you are…"

Nightveil's voice trailed off when she caught sight of her rescuer, but she composed herself quickly.

"uh, hi," she said, trying to hide the awkwardness as she stared into a familiar face from the past. She was less than successful. This was the second Laura Wright she had encountered in as many hours, but this Laura Wright was not Nightveil.

At least not yet.

Nightveil smiled and stuck out her hand. "Laura Wright. A pleasure to meet you."

"How do you know my name?" the gun-wielding heroine known as the Blue Bulleteer asked, suddenly taken aback by this stranger who somehow knew the secret identity she had worked so diligently to keep under wraps.

Nightveil lifted the mask from her face so the other her could see it clearly. "Because it's my name too," she said, trying not to laugh at the absurdity of it all.

"How is this possible?" Blue Bulleteer demanded, her gun still trained on the newcomer.

"It's a long story," Nightveil said. "It's involves alternate dimensions and an attack on the Crossroads of Infinity."

"I don't know what that is," Blue Bulleteer said.

"It's the center of the multiverse… uh, the place where multiple dimensions converge." She pursed her lips, irritated, then tried again. "It's literally the center of everything. Someone is trying to destroy the barrier that keeps our dimensions separate. I tried to stop her, but I wasn't strong enough."

"What happens if this barrier thing of yours breaks?"

Nightveil let out a breath. "If that happens, the myriad dimensions would spill over into one another until there was only one dimension left."

"Sounds horrible."

"You don't know the half of it," Nightveil added. "As the dimensional planes settle in atop one another, the barriers between them will crack like eggshells and they'll wipe one another out. Billions upon billions will die in each dimension, but that's just the beginning. The destruction will ripple outward until there is nothing left. We're talking the end of everything."

"Why am I not surprised?" Blue Bulleteer said with a smirk. "There's always some damn thing or the other in this blamed war!"

"What war?"

"Are you kidding me?"

The Blue Bulleteer motioned upward and Nightveil lifted her eyes. The sky was filled with balloons very much like the one she had run into. They were tethered to the ground so they would not stray from their position. Nightveil had seen this type of strategy used before, in London during World War II, when the Germans continuously strafed the city.

The London Blitz.

"Where are we?" Nightveil asked.

"New York."

"Who are we fighting? Or, perhaps I should ask who is bombing this city?"

The Blue Bulleteer gave her a quizzical look. "You really aren't from around here, are you?"

"Afraid not. I don't even know where here is, at least dimensionally-wise."

"I may have someone who can help with that," Blue Bulleteer said, glancing at her watch. "But first, we need to get you off the street. We're due an attack any minute now."

That's when Nightveil noticed a buzzing sound in the air. It sounded like a nest of angry hornets at first, but as the sound grew closer, she recognized it as the rattle and hum of airplane engines... a lot of them.

"There!" Blue Bulleteer shouted, pointing toward the east.

"My God," Nightveil muttered. "There's so many of them."

Like an angry horde of locusts out of Biblical times, hundreds of Japanese Zeroes filled the evening sky. If they had attacked during the day, they would have blotted out the blue of the sky, but flying in as the sky burned purple, orange, and pink, they were harder to pinpoint by surface to air weaponry.

They flew in low, much the way Nightveil had read of the attack on Pearl Harbor in her dimension. New York's high-rise buildings worked against that strategy here. They were low until they reached the city, but then they had to take air unless the pilots were good enough to navigate between the buildings. Such a feat was not impossible, but it was highly improbable. The most likely outcome would be Zeroes crashing into buildings.

The Zeroes opened fire on the balloons.

The balloons were the only visible impediment to bombs dropped from the planes. Impact with a balloon detonated the explosive high overhead instead of at ground level or inside a building.

Once the enemy planes were in range, gunnery nests that were assembled on the balconies of several of the high-rise buildings opened fire on the enemy aircraft. It was a testament to Yankee American know how. Many planes were knocked out of the sky by the building mounted guns.

After the first pass, the Zeroes retreated back toward the open water from where they came.

"They'll be back," Blue Bulleteer said. "You can count on that."

"I don't understand," Nightveil said. "Those were Japanese Zeroes."

"Yes. Hurry. We must get off the street." The Blue Bulleteer motioned ahead and the women headed for cover.

"Are we at war with Japan?" Nightveil asked once they were on the move.

"For about the last eighty years," Blue Bulleteer said. "Every time we think we've beaten the Axis back, they hole up for a couple of years then come back swinging with upgraded weaponry and a new determination to wipe out the United States and its allies."

"And they've brought the war here to America?"

"Yes. After the fall of London in '63, the United States was the only major super power left to stand against the Axis powers. We're outgunned and outnumbered, but this is where we will make our stand," Blue Bulleteer said. "If we fall here, there's nowhere to fall back to. Not anymore."

She noticed the confused look on Nightveil's face.

"I take it, things played out differently where you come from?" she asked.

"You could say that," Nightveil said. "On my world, none of this happened. World War II ended in 1945."

"Then you are truly fortunate, Laura, to have lived a life free of this infernal war."

"Oh, my dimension has had its fair share of war," Nightveil added. "We've just had momentary stretches of peace between them."

"What tipped the war in your favor?" Blue Bulleteer asked.

"Our side built a bigger weapon... an atomic bomb."

"An atomic..." the Blue Bulleteer's voice trailed off. "Our scientists toyed with the idea decades ago, but they couldn't quite make it work. Plus, there were objections from citizens about the creation of such a weapon. The destructive power of something that powerful would be catastrophic."

"Your scientists were not wrong," Nightveil said as she stepped into an alley at her companion's urging. "The United States dropped their bomb on the Japanese cities of Hiroshima and Nagasaki. The destruction was significant. The loss of life was devastating."

"But it ended the war?"

"It did indeed," Nightveil said.

"Perhaps our leaders should reexamine their plans," Blue Bulleteer said. "I'll make sure that information gets to them."

"Before you pull that trigger, just remember, this is a weapon of mass destruction. The death toll will be extensive," Nightveil said.

"Enough people have already died in this ungodly war. If taking out a few hundred thousand more is the only way to bring about a lasting peace, then it is something that must be considered."

"Maybe. I'm just glad I won't be here to see it."

"You know a way back to your home dimension?"

"Sort of," Nightveil said. "But I'm tired and my power reserves are low. I need to recharge, meditate. Is there someplace quiet we can go?"

The Blue Bulleteer smiled. "I know just the place," she said as her eyes began to glow.

Motioning with her hands, the Blue Bulleteer performed a transportation spell that Nightveil had used herself on occasion. Of course, back when she had been the Blue Bulleteer, spells were not part of her repertoire. Obviously, this version of her had mystical training as well, but for reasons she could only guess, this Laura Wright did not give up the Blue Bulleteer identity to become Nightveil.

This truly was a different dimension.

A transport bubble wrapped around them both, a glowing yellow vortex similar to the one Nightveil still had tucked away for safe keeping within her cape.

"Where are we going?" Nightveil asked.

"To see an old friend," Blue Bulleteer said as

the transport bubble popped them out of New York.

Half a breath later, Nightveil and the Blue Bulleteer reappeared in a place that was at once all too familiar to the visitor from another dimension and yet different enough to not feel like her home.

"Welcome to the Sanctum, Laura," Blue Bulleteer said once they arrived.

"I love what you've done with the place," Nightveil said as she looked around. She ran her gloved finger across the spines of the books. The library was similar to her own, with a few notable exceptions. What she found the most surprising was the amount of dust that had settled on everything and the piles of boxes and odds and ends stacked around the house in a haphazard manner. "I'm guessing you don't live here?"

"No," she said with a laugh. "This is more like my home away from home."

"I stayed here during my training. The wizard wanted me to live here, but I'm a city girl at heart. Plus, I can do more good out there fighting on the front lines than I can sitting here in some stuffy old house in the swamp."

"Was your wizard named Azagoth?"

The Blue Bulleteer smiled. "I'm guessing he was yours as well."

"He was."

"Was yours a cranky old bastard like mine?"

Nightveil barked out a laugh. "He had his moments."

"Moments of greatness, I'm sure," a voice called from another room.

Blue Bulleteer winced.

Nightveil chucked a thumb in the direction of the other room. *Is that...?* she mouthed.

Blue Bulleteer nodded.

Nightveil pursed her lips and waited for them both to be chastised for showing impertinence.

"I didn't know you were home," Blue Bulleteer said. "We have a visitor."

"Join me in the parlor, would you?"

The Blue Bulleteer motioned Nightveil toward the parlor. It was all unnecessary, of course. The layout of the house was identical to her own. There were some things in this world that were constant, no matter which alternate dimension they resided in.

Nightveil did not expect any major surprises inside the sanctum.

She was wrong.

Her Azagoth was an interdimensional being himself. Azagoth was an elder wizard, not constrained to a flesh and blood human body. He was a large floating eye encased in a fur-covered box. Nightveil, and others, had acted as his hands and feet over the centuries.

Nightveil stepped into the parlor expecting to see her mentor in the form with which she was familiar.

Instead of the familiar floating eye in a box, a man stood in the parlor, his back to the entrance as he stared out the window at the Everglades beyond. He wore jeans and had on a leather jacket, despite the Florida heat. He had brown hair.

"Welcome back, my student," the man said with Azagoth's voice.

Then he turned around and looked directly at

Nightveil.

"Or perhaps I should say, *students*?"

Nightveil felt her jaw drop. This was not the Azagoth she knew, but she did know this man. On her plane of reality, this man was an ally, a friend. The only difference with this version was the third eye, Azagoth's eye, in the center of his forehead.

"Charlie?" she asked cautiously.

"No, my dear. I am not Charlie Starrett. I am Azagoth."

"How is this possible?" Nightveil asked. "You look just like Charlie."

"Charlie and Azagoth were both injured a couple of years back in an attack by a Rurian warlord named Proxima," Blue Bulleteer said, laying a comforting arm on her counterpart's shoulder. "They stopped the invaders, but their injuries were too severe. We almost lost both of them until a radical idea was suggested."

"Azagoth and Charlie merged together? How is that possible?"

"It's not quite that simple," Blue Bulleteer tried to explain.

Azagoth gave her a sad smile. "I'm afraid the man you knew as Captain Paragon is dead."

7.

Laura Wright woke with a start.

At first, she wondered if it had all been a dream. Had she really come to an alternate Earth in a dimension where World War II never ended, where she never taken the name Nightveil, and where her mentor, the wizard Azagoth inhabited the body of the man she had once known as Captain Paragon.

It all seemed so fantastical that it did not feel real even though she knew it was true.

"Feeling better?" Azagoth asked with Captain Paragon's voice.

"How long was I out?"

"You have been asleep for about five hours."

"The fight must have taken more out of me than I thought."

"You appeared exhausted," Azagoth said.

He was sitting in a rocking chair in the corner of the room next to a small table filled with books and a small plate of fruit and a box of her favorite cereal. He looked comfortable. After she woke, he closed the book he had been reading and sat it on the table. She noted, with some amusement, that he was reading the same book she had finished before all of the day's craziness had started for her.

"This is all a little hard to take," Nightveil said as she slowly eased herself into a seated position.

She was sore all over from the fight and the crash.

"Which part?"

"The war. The other me in there. You! Take your pick."

"I apologize for that, Laura," Azagoth said. "I can only imagine how difficult an adjustment this is for you."

She swung her feet out from under the covers and off the bed, surprised to find that she was no longer wearing her costume. That was when she noticed her arms were also bare.

"You undressed me?" she said through grit teeth, trying to bite back her anger.

"No," the face of Charlie Starrett said with a sly smile. She still had trouble reconciling that it was Azagoth in there and not the man she knew as Captain Paragon. "Laura... our Laura undressed you after you passed out."

"Passed out?"

"You were quite exhausted and you had just fallen from a rather great height," Azagoth said. "Your uniform was rather... well, that is to say it needed a good laundering. Laura thought it would be less awkward if she removed your clothes to wash them. They are lying there on the nightstand next to the bed."

"First of all," Nightveil started. "Nothing about this whole twisted affair is less awkward."

She twirled her fingers and magically reassembled the molecules of her costume so that it disappeared from the nightstand and reassembled on her body. She got out of bed and stretched, her costume back in place save for the mask.

"Secondly, thank you for the clean uniform."

"My pleasure," Azagoth said. He motioned toward the food on the table next to him. "Hungry? It's not much, but I'm happy to share."

Nightveil joined him at the table. The plate contained a slice of watermelon, strawberries, grapes, and a couple of slices of tomato. She picked up the cereal and looked at the ingredients, suddenly worried about her carb intake.

"I'm sorry there's no milk," Azagoth said. "Our supply lines were recently cut so we've been unable to procure any perishables for a couple of weeks. The fruit and vegetables are grown locally. We have several small greenhouses around the city in converted apartments.

"How very industrious of you," Nightveil said. "Why can't you or Laura simple..." she opened her hand quickly in a *POOF!* maneuver. "You know, pop over to a neighboring dimension for some food and weapons?"

"Dimensional breaches are not as easy as they once were," Azagoth said. "The other side has a powerful mystic on their side. We don't know who it is, but whoever it is, they've placed some kind of dampening field around the city. No interdimensional travel. Leaving the city is difficult as well. Between frequent air raids and roving patrols, moving about the city is tough. Leaving the city is downright impossible. We're stuck here."

Azagoth laid a hand on hers.

"And, I'm sorry to say, my dear, but so are you."

Nightveil shook her head. "But I came here

through a dimensional breach. One minute, I was in the wasteland outside the Crossroads of Infinity. The next, I was here."

"Are you certain?"

"Yes. There is a way, Azagoth. We simply have to find it."

"What is the first thing you remember when you arrived in this dimension?"

"Falling."

"From an airplane?"

"I don't think so," Nightveil said, replaying the events in her mind. "I'm pretty sure I was thrown in here by the woman I was fighting. I was pretty high up there though."

She snapped her fingers as the answer came to her.

"The dampening field has a height limit!" she shouted.

Azagoth smiled and slapped a hand down on the table. The action sent grapes and strawberries rolling off the plate.

"Laura!" he shouted. He looked back at Nightveil. Not you. Uh, my Laura."

"I guessed as much," Nightveil said as she grabbed a grape before it went over the edge of the table. She popped it in her mouth. It tasted sweet.

Like victory.

***

After Nightveil filled in the Blue Bulleteer and Azagoth on her theory and her plan, they hit the streets.

New York City was in flames. Pillars of smoke curled into the air in every direction she looked. Even though the events around her had never happened on her Earth, Nightveil was all too familiar with what an attack on this city looked like She had hoped to never see this magnificent city in flames again.

"Does it look that different to you?" Blue Bulleteer asked once they settled into position on the balcony of a bombed out apartment building while they waited for their back up to arrive. Water leaked through the large hole where the roof had once stood.

"Is it that obvious?"

"Yeah. At least to me. I'm guessing your world has had some advances that we haven't quite gotten around to yet."

"Something like that," Nightveil said. "The New York I know is shiny and bright. There's plasma screens all over the city with their advertisements and twenty-four hour news channels."

"Sounds absolutely horrible," Blue Bulleteer said. "How does anyone sleep?"

Nightveil laughed. "I guess you get used to it, Laura," she said. "I still live in Florida, but my New York is actually quite lovely. I visit as often as I can."

"I'll take your word for it."

"We get done with this and I may just have to take you there for a visit."

Blue Bulleteer's mood hardened. She sighed. "After the war, okay?"

"It's a deal," Nightveil said. "I appreciate you

taking time away to help me with this… this…"

"Harebrained plan?"

"Yeah. That."

"Well, this crisis affects us too. I'll join you, but we should try to get back here as fast as we can. I hate to leave everyone in the lurch."

"I know exactly how you feel. How long until our back up arrives?"

Blue Bulleteer looked at her watch. "We've got a few minutes."

"Good."

"Do you really think your enemy is guarding the rift?"

"I don't know," Nightveil said. "I wouldn't put it past her so better safe than sorry."

"Always a good plan."

"As soon as I've gathered a few more allies, I'll send for you and yours."

"I know the plan."

"Your problem is going to be getting up there to that breach."

"You just leave that to me," Blue Bulleteer said with a sly wink. "I'm cooking up a plan to take care of that little problem."

"Things are looking up already," Nightveil joked.

The Blue Bulleteer waggled her hand "*maybe*." She seemed less enthusiastic about the plan than her cohort.

"A few more fighters on our side and I think we can defeat the enemy," Nightveil added, trying to reassure her other self.

"You never told me who this enemy is," Blue

Bulleteer said.

"No. I didn't, did I"

"Any particular reason why not?"

"It's hard to find the words," Nightveil said. "If I say it out loud, it's real and I really wish it wasn't real."

"Okay, after than build up, you can't not tell me. Who is it?"

"It's me," Nightveil said. She waggled a finger back and forth between them. "It's us. Another version of Laura Wright."

"How is that possible?"

"As I understand it, every time someone makes a decision, there are multiple outcomes they can choose. For each decision made, a divergent reality is created. It sounds crazy, I know."

"Crazy is an understatement."

"Welcome to my world," Nightveil said.

"How many of these... what did you call them... divergent realities are there?" Blue Bulleteer asked.

Nightveil shrugged.

"How many decisions have ever been made in the history of the world?"

Blue Bulleteer whistled.

"That many, huh?"

"Probably more than either of us can comprehend," Nightveil said.

"And why, exactly, does this other version of us want to destroy all of these other realities you mentioned?"

"I don't know," Nightveil said. "Your guess is as good as mine, but I assure you that's one of the questions I'm planning to ask her right after we stop her."

"And this help you're going off to recruit?"

Nightveil smiled. "I figure the best way to take down one evil Laura Wright is with a whole bunch of good Laura Wrights."

"Strength in numbers, eh?" Blue Bulleteer said.

"Something like that."

Blue Bulleteer looked down Broadway.

"Uh, Laura, what are some of the effects of the dimensional walls breaching again?"

"Bleed through is the most common," Nightveil said. "Objects or places from one dimension sometimes slip through the cracks and wind up in their neighboring dimension. Sometimes it happens without anyone noticing because they're both similar. Other times, it's like… well, imagine if a B-12 Bomber showed up in Camelot."

"That would certainly be an attention getter," Blue Bulleteer said. "I guess seeing a dinosaur in a modern city would be an indication too, right?"

"Sure. That's a good example," Nightveil said.

She stopped and looked at her counterpart.

"That's a pretty specific example. What do you…"

Blue Bulleteer tugged on Nightveil's cape then pointed to the street below.

"Does that count as bleed through?"

"I'm guessing that's not normal here?" Nightveil asked.

"Uh uh." Blue Bulleteer shook her head.

"Then, yeah, I'd say that definitely counts!"

Below them, a herd of dinosaurs ran down the

street. Nightveil immediately recognized them as Triceratops. They were each around ten feet tall, thirty feet long, and they probably weighed ten or fifteen tons a piece. With their hard, scaly skin and armor knocking anything and everything in their path out of the way, they resembled a herd of tanks clearing a path down Broadway and leaving destruction in their wake.

Thankfully, the street was deserted in anticipation for the coming air raid.

"I guess that's one thing to be thankful for," Blue Bulleteer said. "Never thought I'd be happy for a blitz run."

"At least we got the plant eating variety," Nightveil observed. "Unless our scientists got it wrong."

"Or they evolved differently in that other dimension they come from."

"Now you're getting it," Nightveil added.

"I'm more concerned with why they're running," Blue Bulleteer said. "It looks like there's something chasing after them."

"Oh, I wish you hadn't said that," Nightveil said a half a second before the all too familiar roar of a Tyrannosaurus Rex as it rounded the corner and followed its would-be dinner onto Broadway. "I was kind of hoping that wouldn't happen!"

"Well, this day just gets better and better," Blue Bulleteer said.

"You'll get no argument from me," Nightveil added.

Nightveil was on the move, her cape sweeping high into the air as she leapt off the balcony into the air. "I'll take care of the T-Rex! Can you corral those guys?"

"I'm on it," Blue Bulleteer shouted as she leapt off the balcony.

As she dropped, her form began to grow, to change. It was a power that Nightveil had also, though not one she used with any regularity. She assumed her doppelganger was much the same way. The pain of transmogrification from normal human size to giant size was not overwhelming, but neither was it pleasant. She held her giantess form in reserve and used it only when she felt there was no other choice.

When she reached the ground, the Blue Bulleteer stood easily seventy feet tall. Her costume stretched with her, presumably aided by magic, Nightveil guessed. Not that there was a lot of costume there to begin with. She often wondered why she had thought such a skimpy outfit was a good idea back when she wore the mantle of Blue Bulleteer, back before she met Azagoth and became Nightveil. Outside of distracting her enemies, there were times it was more hassle than anything else. Especially in the winter.

Gods, I hope she remembered to put on underwear!

Blue Bulleteer ran ahead of the beasts, pushing cars and wrecks that had once been recognizable as automobiles into walls to create a barrier that she could use to lead them where she needed them to go.

As long as they don't barrel ahead and tear right through these hunks of metal like they're tinfoil.

She hated the thought as soon as it popped into her brain. If she couldn't herd the dinos into a pen that could hold them, she was screwed.

Too bad I can't sic 'em on the enemy, she thought.

The buildings in this particular borough were mostly empty thanks to constant shelling in the area, which had forced the residents to evacuate and head deeper inland where enemy attacks happened with less efficiency. The enemy's hit and run tactics had one big disadvantage, the Zeroes had very limited fuel supplies to keep them light and fast. After blitzing the city, there was not enough fuel to reach inland and return home.

Without having to worry about civilian casualties, corralling the wild dinosaurs -*still can't believe I'm seeing this*- in one of the vacated tenements was her best bet. Step One was getting them off the street, which was no easy task. The last thing she needed was the enemy to realize that there were dinosaurs run amok in the city. Based on some of the things she had already witnessed in the incredibly lengthy war, the enemy would probably try to capture and weaponize the beasts.

That's the last thing any of us needs!

The triceratops appeared to be as frightened of her as she was of them so, surprisingly, all it took was a gentle nudge to convince them to turn where she wanted them to and herd them onto a cross street and then into a bombed out apartment building. The walls of the structure were still sound, but a bomb hit directly on the roof had caused a massive collapse that all but gutted the center of the brick and steel edifice.

New York was literally littered with buildings like this one, a scar from a war without end.

Once they were inside to confines of the building, she slid cars in front of the door then with a magical assist, stacked others on top of them before melting them together into am immoveable pile of slag to bar the doors and shore up the walls. Her spell work wasn't as advanced as Nightveil's, but the Blue Bulleteer's mystic training had begun under the tutelage of the wizard, Azagoth before he merged with Captain Paragon. It was a slow process as fighting the war took precedence over learning how to float a pencil.

Her mystic welding job would hold the beasts for a short time until her more powerful doppelganger showed up to finish the job. She had no doubt that Nightveil could erect a more permanent solution regarding their displaced guests.

While the Blue Bulleteer corralled the triceratops herd, Nightveil grabbed the attention of the dinosaur that was chasing them. She took to the air and stayed out of the T-Rex's reach. While it's claws were close to its body, the sharp teeth in its mighty muscled jaws and tail that swung like a wrecking ball, were another matter. They gave the predator a longer reach and from what she could see of them in action, she knew this T-Rex was an experienced hunter. With her protection spells in place, it was possible that she could withstand a strike from either the jaws or the tail, but she really wasn't looking to put that to the test.

"It's been a long time since I saw a big lizard like you, Rexxy baby," she joked. Humor helped keep her focused. "He tried to make a meal out of me too. You guys are all alike. No class at all."

Purple bolts flew from her outstretched hands, peppering the monster like hundreds of BBs from a pellet gun. The T-Rex was smart. He turned his face from the barrage and swung at the attacking pests with its mighty muscled tail. Had the attacks been anything other than mystical bolts, the strategy would have worked.

Nightveil pressed the attack, pushing the dinosaur into retreat.

"Now I've got you," she muttered as she gave chase.

Placing her hands together, thumbs interlocked, Nightveil unleashed a powerful binding spell. The beams that erupted from her hands sent a bright pink glowing band of energy at the T-Rex, who tried to outrun it, but failed. Not even its top speed was faster than the speed of thought magic.

The glowing band enveloped the prehistoric visitor in their stronger than steel grip and held it in place. The dinosaur struggled to free itself from the prison, but in spite of the extra strain, Nightveil held firm.

"Now, where can we put you that's out of the way?"

She saw the giant Blue Bulleteer wave from the next block over and she headed toward her giantess with her new pet in tow. The T-Rex roared with anger as it was lifted off the ground and flown across the city, held aloft by pink bands of energy from a being so much smaller than he. *King of the jungle no more, eh, Rexxy?*

"That looks like a good place. What do you think?" she asked her passenger, who roared his indignance.

"Yeah. Yeah. Just hold your socks, Rex," she said. "We'll have you on the ground in a minute."

Her giant friend pointed her in the right direction and Nightveil dropped through the hole in the roof with her passenger in tow. Below her, the herd of triceratops went into a mad frenzy when they saw their predator enter, but there was nowhere for them to go.

Nightveil found a section of the second floor that was still intact and placed the angry dinosaur there. Before she released her grip, she used her magicks to reinforce the walls and floor to keep the beast caged.

Once the T-Rex was safely tucked away, Nightveil headed to the first floor where she created a corral for the scared triceratops so they wouldn't trample one another trying to escape. A simple relaxation spell and they settled down a bit.

"I'm surprised that worked," Blue Bulleteer said.

"That makes two of us."

Nightveil clapped her hands together as if knocking away dust.

"That should keep them in place for a little while," she said. "At least until we can find a way to get them back home."

"Home?"

Nightveil smirked. "Well, wherever they came

from. I'm not zoned for pets where I live."

They both laughed at the lackluster attempt at humor.

"This is not something we see around here every day, that's for sure," Blue Bulleteer said, still having trouble believing the evidence of her eyes, hands, and nose. *Those beasts stink!*

"I imagine not," Nightveil said.

The Blue Bulleteer looked at her watch. "We need to move. Back up is on the way and our diversion is about to start."

"Let's go."

"If this doesn't work..." Blue Bulleteer started as she shrunk back to her normal size.

"It will."

"Well, just in case it doesn't, it's been a pleasure meeting you, Laura."

"Same to you, Laura," Nightveil said. "Ready?"

"As I'll ever be."

"Hold on."

Nightveil took the Blue Bulleteer by the hand and the two of them gently lifted into the air. The Blue Bulleteer knew how to handle an airplane and had flown more than her fair share of missions for the War Department, but flying under her own power was a skill Azagoth had not yet taught her. That was something that would have to be rectified soon, she decided. She found it equally thrilling and terrifying as they hovered amidst the balloons that covered the city.

"Hold tight."

"Don't worry."

"Here they come," Nightveil said.

Sure enough, a squadron of Japanese Zeroes headed for the city on its next attack run. Once they were in range, the zeroes opened fire on the balloons. It was a tried and true strategy that had implemented multiple times before.

It was usually successful.

Not this time.

With a magical push, Nightveil hurled the Blue Bulleteer toward the planes.

She started to grow as soon as Nightveil released her hand.

By the time she reached them, the Blue Bulleteer was once again a giant. She grabbed hold of the building Nightveil had picked out for her and grabbed one of the planes, plucking it right out of the sky.

Using the plane's engines and momentum against it, threw it toward the ground.

The Zero exploded on impact.

The Blue Bulleteer laughed as she reached out for her next target.

That was Nightveil's cue. She launched herself skyward at full speed, making best possible speed toward the dimensional breach. On her way up, she tossed off several force bolts at the attacking planes. She took out two of them and smiled when she saw the remainder of the squadron turn tail and retreat.

Hopefully, that will buy you some breathing room, Laura, Nightveil thought as she approached the breach.

She closed her eyes and said a silent prayer.

Nightveil plunged headfirst into the breach--

--and vanished.

8.

Laura Wright found herself once more in the wasteland.

She tumbled out of the breach, disoriented and off balance. Flying out of the breach at top speed, she dropped to her knees and rolled twice, her extremities tingling on contact with the desert floor.

Nightveil recovered quickly and got to her feet. She had to escape the discomfort. A simple spell broke contact with gravity and she hovered an inch above the Wasteland, once again severing her connection to the painful energy spikes.

With the barriers between dimensions weakened as they were, she thought it best not to press her luck by leaping from one to the other under her own power, which was no easy task even under the best of circumstances. She feared that doing so might possibly speed up the deterioration that her evil counterpart had already set in motion. Nightveil refused to act in such a reckless manner. That meant she would have to use the breaches that already existed and sneak in and out of them like a thief through an open kitchen window. It was risky, but she saw no other alternative.

The real trick with moving between dimensions this way was avoiding contact with the Nightveil who was the cause of the catastrophe befalling the multiverse.

That would take guile and subterfuge.

These were not Nightveil's best skills, but she wasn't exactly a novice at this sort of thing either. She would simply have to be careful and not...

"I thought I had gotten rid of you."

...not be spotted.

Damn!

The chaos seemed worse as the sky above the desert wasteland had begun to darken. Colors still exploded into flowery shapes, but the colors were more muted, as if being viewed through dark sunglasses. The Crossroads of Infinity had dimmed. Was it dying? There was no way to know. This was uncharted territory for her and she suddenly wished that Azagoth was there to tell her how to solve the problem.

"Well, this is a surprise," the other woman said.

The woman she had come to think of as evil Nightveil hovered above her, the dark colors of her costume blending into the chaos that filled the night sky. Save for the thin glow of her amplified power that surrounded her, she would have blended seamlessly into the background. Chaos energy popped and crackled around her clenched fists. She was ready to finish the fight they had begun the last time Nightveil ventured into the wasteland.

Nightveil, on the other hand, wasn't ready for round two, but she needed to buy herself some time to find another breach.

"I really didn't think you had the stones to come back here," evil Nightveil said.

"The union would take away my superhero card

if I didn't try my best to stop you and your crazy scheme," Nightveil said, projecting bravado to mask her unease. It was a common practice for those in her line of work.

"Crazy? Laura, Laura, Laura, you poor, pitiful soul. How can you be so narrowminded?" the evil one said. "Have you not noticed... well, no, I guess you haven't... but with each dimensional offshoot that is created, the core dimension, my dimension, is diminished."

"How so?"

"You wouldn't understand."

Nightveil couldn't help but laugh. "You're probably right, but then again, I'm not crazy."

"Time to say goodbye, Laura," evil Nightveil said.

"I couldn't agree more," Nightveil said as she spotted a fresh breach nearby

She leapt toward the breach without preamble and was through the dimensional doorway before her evil counterpart could react.

I just hope she doesn't follow me, Nightveil thought as she tumbled through the vortex into darkness.

***

The sun was setting when Nightveil reached her destination.

Moving on the fly as she did, there had been no time to recon the dimension or make sure it was safe. This time, the breach opened closer to the ground. She tumbled out only a foot above solid ground. Training kicked in and she landed in a roll that came up into a crouch, ready for battle if an attack came. She had to remember to thank Ms. Victory for the advanced combat training when she got back home.

Okay, so where are we this time?

Her surroundings certainly felt familiar. The unmistakable twang of swamp water hit her almost instantly. At least that was one mystery easily solved. She was back home in the Everglades. No other swamp she had ever visited could match the musty aroma of her home swamp.

Be it ever so humble.

She looked skyward and gasped when she saw the blood red sky above.

With a thought, gravity released its hold and she soared skyward, curious what could make the sky change color from the blue of her Earth to the deep red of this one. She hoped the sanctum would provide her with answers.

Once she was above the tall pines and Cyprus trees that dotted the wetland landscape, she looked for a familiar energy signature. Back home, her sanctum was not visible from above so she had no reason to believe the one belonging to the Nightveil or Azagoth of this dimension would be any different. A simple cloaking spell kept unwanted visitors from her door unless they happened to walk right up on the old Victorian house that hovered a few feet above the swampy waters.

Nightveil was no simple visitor.

And she had more ways of looking than her eyes.

Eyes closed, her breathing steady, Nightveil reached out with her senses. She plucked at errant stands, getting a lay of the land as her mind brushed through the mystical nerve clusters of the Everglades.

Based on what she had found on the last world she visited, Nightveil was surprised to find this dimension almost identical to her own, the color of the sky notwithstanding.

There you are!

The sanctum located, Nightveil rode the leisurely air currents toward her home away from home until she saw it below.

She floated a few feet from the front porch, a precaution in case the lady of the house had set in place lethal countermeasures that might recognize that she wasn't native to this dimension. This *was* her house, but at the same time, it wasn't. She was the trespasser here so it was paramount that she be cautious.

"Hello!" she called out, cupping her hands over her mouth like a megaphone.

No answer.

Inching closer to the porch, she kept her senses tuned to any potential danger. As near as she could tell, everything about this sanctum felt right... normal. Once she was over the porch she allowed gravity to resume its hold on her and gingerly landed on the stained wood. Remembering that, appearances to the contrary, this was not her home, she did the polite thing and knocked on the door.

No answer.

She knocked again.

Only silence greeted her from inside.

Slowly, she turned the handle, not surprised to find it unlocked for her. This might not be her home dimension, but she was still Laura Wright and the sanctum knew her.

The door opened with only the tiniest of squeaks to announce the new arrival.

"Anyone home?"

She took in the smells and sounds of the sanctum. It felt right, an earthy musty scent like a combination of a spice shop and a shack built in the middle of a swamp. Everything was still, which was off putting. Her own home was constantly abuzz with magic. It filled the rooms like air and vibrated in the walls. The static energy goose-pimpled her flesh as she moved from room to room. It made her feel alive.

This sanctum was as silent as a tomb and she wondered for a moment, if she had inadvertently found the home dimension of the Laura Wright who was even at that moment trying to destroy the barrier that kept the dimensions separated.

She quickly dismissed that notion. It would be the height of coincidence to have found the one dimensional frequency of her enemy based on a lucky guess. That would be the ultimate Hail Mary and Nightveil was not a big believer in coincidence.

This is spooky, she thought as she moved through the empty old house. *What could have happened here to silence the magic? Is my counterpart from this dimension dead?*

She recalled the bodies littering the wasteland, the victims of her other self. Could the Laura

Wright who lived here have been one of them? It was possible.

Damn! I'll find no help here.

Nightveil took one last look then headed for the door. She was on a clock and if there was no help to be found here, then she would have to move on to find allies elsewhere.

She stepped onto the porch and froze.

Standing calf-deep in the swampy waters in front of the sanctum stood several men and women, locals from the look of them. They carried torches and flashlights. All were armed, either with farm tools, baseball bats, or guns.

Something tells me this isn't the local welcoming wagon.

"Uh, hi there," she said, trying to keep the nervousness from her voice. "Can I help you with something?"

She cringed, the words sounding silly even as she said them aloud.

An older gentleman stepped forward, limping as he maneuvered through the thick muck. He held a flaming torch in his left hand and had a shotgun braced on his right arm. He wore waders over jeans and a button up red flannel shirt. A faded brown vest and trucker cap completed the ensemble.

Nightveil did not recognize him.

"It's true," he said, almost reverently. "You've returned. At long last, you've returned to us!"

Uh oh!

"I think you might have me mistaken for someone else," Nightveil said.

"Are you not the high priestess of Azagoth?" the

man asked.

"High priestess?" The words were hard to say, much less believe. "No. I am not her. I'm sorry. I'm called Nightveil."

"So was the high priestess."

"I suspected as much, but I assure you, I am not her. I'm... uh... I'm from out of town."

"But you wear her cloak. You come from inside her home."

She tried to deflect the conversation. "Yes. I, too was looking for your high priestess. I've come seeking her aid, but she is not here."

"So, you stole her cloak?"

"What?" She held up the cloak by its edge. "No. This one is mine. I brought it with me from... *how do I explain this?*... from the place where I come from."

Oh, yeah. That explains it.

"Did the butcher, Azagoth send you?" the old man asked. "Are you a harbinger for his return?"

Using the words *butcher* and *harbinger* did not fill her with a sense that the Azagoth of this dimension was the benevolent being she knew and loved. Her Azagoth had his moments where he was a royal pain to deal with, but most of the time he had her best interests at heart, even if he didn't always show it. Apparently, that was not the case on this world.

"No," she said, playing it smart. "I was not sent by Azagoth. I am... I am a traveler from an alternate dimension. I came here seeking aid from your protector to stop a great evil that threatens us all."

"What is this great evil's name?" a woman shouted from the crowd.

"I was afraid you were going to ask that," Nightveil muttered. "The great evil's name is also Nightveil. She's a villain from another reality that…"

It was no use. The crowd was no longer listening. They surged forward as one, an angry mob out for her head.

Nightveil took a step back, ready to defend herself. Unfortunately, she had been so focused on the mob that she did not notice the men sneaking up on her porch from the opposite side.

"Behind you!" a voice screamed from the crowd.

The warning came too late as a baseball bat grazed the side of her head, knocking Nightveil off balance. She fell against the porch railing, but in the sanctum's state of disrepair, the wood was weak and couldn't hold her weight. It snapped like a twig and sent her sprawling into the dirty swamp water with a splash.

The mob was on her before she had a chance to regroup.

Instinct and training helped her deflect the blows from the angry villagers, but she needed a moment of clear thinking to erect a spell that would free her.

With a thought, she formed a force bubble that pushed her attackers away, if only by a foot. With them out of arm's reach, she got to her feet, unsteady, but she backed against a tree for support. The breather put Nightveil in a better position to fight or flee. With the fate of thousands upon thousands of realities at stake, she chose to exercise the better part of valor.

Before she could take to the air, a woman slammed into her, tackling her once again into the swampy waters.

The tackle saved her life as a blast from a shotgun splintered the tree she had been leaning against. If she had still been standing there, the blast would have cut her in half.

"Teleport! Now!" the red-headed woman screamed in Nightveil's ear. "Get us out of here!"

Without thought, Nightveil closed her eyes and initiated a mystic teleport. The woman, holding onto her tightly, rode shotgun on the trip. Teleport was a tricky spell, but one of the ones she had learned early on in her career. She had envisioned a place she knew to be a safe haven on her world and that's where the spell would take her.

She only hoped it was on this one as well.

9.

Nightveil felt her guts tighten seconds before she completed the jump.

She and her companion hit the ground hard, knocking the wind from both of them. Nightveil took the brunt of it, landing first, her back slamming into the hardpacked earth.

Her erstwhile traveling companion fell atop her.

"Okay, get off of me," Nightveil said as she pushed the woman away.

That's when she got her first good look at the woman's face.

"Hello, Laura," Nightveil said, finding herself once more face to face with an alternate version of Laura Wright.

Unlike her own raven dark hair, this Laura Wright was a redhead, though clearly not a natural one. With a huff, she got to her feet.

"You guys really do have a thing for red here, don't you?" Nightveil said, pointing at her counterpart's hair and cloak then looking up to the red skies above.

"Oh, you have no idea," Laura said.

"Why were you hiding from those clowns?" Nightveil asked, standing up and dusting herself off.

Laura held up a hand and swirled it with a flourish as though she was about to unleash a spell.

Nothing happened.

"No powers?" Nightveil asked.

"No powers."

"How did that happen?"

Laura stretched, worked out the kinks in her back as she looked around. "I picked a fight with a magician stronger than me," she said. "She stole my powers."

"She?"

"I don't know," Laura said. "She was dressed in dark colors from head to toe. She wore a blood red cloak and her voice was distorted. I never got a good look."

"I'm sorry," Nightveil said.

"I've been trying to find a way to get my powers back, but haven't had much luck."

"I'm sorry," Nightveil said.

"Cutter's Park," Laura said, changing the subject when she finally figured out where they were.

"Yeah. This place always felt safe when I was little. Old Man Cutter would keep this small park behind his house clean. He even set up a swing set."

Laura pointed to the swing set nearby. "Looks like there are some constants in the universe." She walked over and dropped down in one of the swings.

Nightveil took a seat in the swing opposite her.

"I've not thought about this place in years," Laura said.

"Neither have I, but teleporting blind is scary so I picked a safe place from my memory."

"Good call."

"So, let me see if I have this right," Nightveil said. "To hide from the angry mob, you joined the angry mob?"

"To be fair, they aren't always angry."

"I'll have to take your word for it."

"Why are you here?" Laura asked.

"There's trouble."

"There's always trouble."

"Big trouble."

"That too."

"Are you familiar with the Crossroads of Infinity?"

"Of course."

"An alternate version of... well, of us is trying to destroy it and bleed the various dimensions together into one."

"Why would we... uh, she... uh, do that? It doesn't make sense."

"No, it doesn't. I tried to ask her, but she kicked my ass instead."

"How does that get you here?"

"I need help. I'm trying to recruit an army of..."

She laughed.

"An army of Nightveils to stop her."

Laura chuckled. "It takes a Nightveil to stop a Nightveil. That's your plan?"

"Something like that."

"I wish I could help you," Laura said. "But I don't have enough power left in me to float a pencil, much less fight a war."

"Damn," Nightveil said softly.

"I'm sorry."

"Not your fault. I was just hoping for help. So

far, it's just me and a version of me that's still the Blue Bulleteer. Not much of an army yet, but she's also out recruiting."

"You know, I may be able to help you out after all," Laura said, snapping her fingers.

"How's that?"

"You ever visit *Magic Maggie's*?"

"What's a Magic Maggie?"

"Only the coolest bar at the Edge of Infinity."

"I have no idea what that is," Nightveil said.

Laura smiled.

Nightveil recognized that mischievous grin. "Sounds like fun," she said.

"Oh, it is."

"If it's near the Edge of Infinity, then won't the enemy know about it? She's been racking up quite a body count in the wasteland."

"Only one way to find out," Laura said.

"Oh, no. I can't risk it. You don't have any powers. I can't take you into a dangerous situation unarmed."

"But I know where it is," Laura said. "Besides, who said I was going unarmed."

Off Nightveil's surprised look, Laura laughed.

"One more local teleport then we can head for Magic Maggie's."

"Where do you need to go?"

"I've got some shopping to do," Laura said.

***

They reappeared in familiar surroundings.

"First floor, sanctum, weapons, and lady's

94

lingerie," Nightveil joked. "Everybody off."

"Stay quiet," Laura said with a shush. "Our friends are probably still camped out outside, trying to figure out a way to get in here."

Nightveil whispered an easy incantation and a small globe of light illuminated the room around them.

"What are they after in here?" she asked.

Laura smirked. "The sanctum may be drained, but I've stored a lot of weaponry here over the years. You know how it is."

She chucked a thumb toward the front door.

"They want the weapons to use against Azaroth in case he returns."

"Is your Azagoth really that bad?"

"You mean yours isn't?" Laura asked.

"Well, he can be a dick at times, but…"

"My Azagoth tried to enslave the planet."

"Yeah. I can see where that would make him public enemy number one."

"There's a lot of powerful artifacts I ran across when I had your job," Laura said. "Leaving them loose in the world wasn't really an option."

"Understood. I've run across a few odds and ends that needed to be tucked away for safe keeping over the years. What have you got?"

"This," she said as she pulled a large oversized glove from a closet. The silvery glove was three times larger than her hand and it sparkled in the light.

"What's that do?"

"You don't have one of these?"

"Nope."

Laura smiled. "This is the Glove of Rex. It allows me to wield this."

She pulled a staff from the closet with the gloved hand. Nightveil could feel pure unfiltered energy coursing through it. It was almost as tall as Laura, silver in color, similar to the glove, but not sparkly. At the top of the staff was a globe. Faint sparks flared and popped off of it like static electricity.

"Well, that's impressive," Nightveil said.

"I think so."

"What is it?"

"This is the staff of Doominus Rex."

Nightveil shrugged.

"Seriously? You don't even have this guy on your world?"

"He isn't ringing any bells," Nightveil said. "Sorry."

Laura shook her head.

"I take it he was tough?"

"You could say that," Laura said. "It took the combined might of me, Mr. Victory, and the Sentinels of Justice to take him down. We lost two Sentinels in that showdown."

"Mr. Victory?"

"Not even him, huh?"

"Nope. We do have a Ms. Victory. She's leader of a group called F.E.M.Force."

"Never heard of 'em," Laura said.

"They'll be so disappointed," Nightveil said. "Are you ready to travel?"

"Yes. This is what I came for."

"Then hold on to your hat, sister because we are

gone."

With that, Nightveil teleported them away, once more plunging the sanctum into quiet darkness.

10.

Magic Maggie's was nothing like Nightveil expected.

She had heard tales of hidden bars scattered around the dimensional lay lines that catered to mystics, sorcerers, and charlatans, but this was her first time actually visiting one. Not that she had a problem with bars, but her idea of down time did not include tossing back shots and talking shop with others magic users.

Maybe I'm just anti-social.

She had expected shining columns, polished white tiles, magic on full display, things like that. The reality, however, fell far short of her expectations.

Magic Maggie's could be best described as a dive bar. The hardwood floor was littered with peanut shells and puddles of stale beer that, over time, had turned the wood a dark amber the color of molasses. The bar itself nearly matched the floor in color and consistency from years of use and abuse. Knicks and gouges littered the edge of the bar. The walls looked to be at least a couple hundred years old as did the pool tables with their faded felt covers and pool balls with the numbers missing.

"You sure we're in the right place?"

"Absolutely," Laura said as she headed for the

bar, still brandishing the staff of Doominus Rex in her gloved right hand.

Nightveil managed to hide her amusement as the guys who looked like badass bikers opted to find other seats when they saw her coming. Like herself, the staff-wielding Laura Wright was a thin woman, but power recognizes power and with that staff in hand, she was hard to miss.

Nightveil took in the room. The place was packed with magic users in every nook and cranny of the oddly shaped bar. There were tiny alcoves along the far wall with booths inside of them and dangling beads that served as a semi-privacy curtain. She didn't see anyone she knew in the place, but a few of the patrons stood out to her, some famous for their exploits among the magical community and others infamous for much the same reason.

There were even a few non-human customers, which she found fascinating. Nightveil had certainly met an alien or two in her time, but to see aliens and humans coexisting peacefully, even having fun together, was, she had to admit, pretty darn cool.

"Pardon me," a deep baritone voice said as a guy in a red and gold cape bumped into her. She let it go with a "no problem" and moved deeper into the bar.

"There sure are a lot of capes in here," someone said from a nearby table.

"You got something against capes?" Nightveil asked, letting hers flutter open as if it were going to swallow them whole.

"Not at all," the drunk stammered. "Just making

a polite observation."

She gave him a wink and moved on. That's when she saw her traveling companion wave to her from the bar where she motioned for Nightveil to join her.

"Is Mags here?" she asked the bartender as Nightveil slid onto the stool next to her.

"She's in the back."

"Tell her Laura Wright is here and that she would like a word."

"A word?" the bartender sneered.

"Maybe two words."

The bartender stared her down, lifted an eyebrow in a manner that would have made Leonard Nimoy proud.

"It's important," Laura said, emphasizing each word.

The bartender started to fire off another snarky remark, but then he glanced at the staff and decided against it, which was probably the smartest move he could have made. "Let me see if she's taking visitors today," he said instead before ducking around the corner toward the back office.

"Good service is so hard to find these days," Laura said as she leaned over the bar and pulled a bottle from beneath the counter."

She held up the bottle, stared at the amber liquid inside, and smiled.

"The good stuff."

Nightveil smiled. She liked this version of herself. She was sassy.

"Conjure us up a glass or two, would you?" Laura asked.

Nightveil gestured and two glasses shimmered into view on the bar top.

"Impressive," Laura said with an amused grin.

Nightveil shrugged. "Kid's stuff."

"But impressive kid's stuff," Laura joked as she popped the cork on the bottle.

She poured a small amount in each glass before recorking the bottle.

The ladies held up their glasses and clinked them before taking a sip.

Nightveil was cautious. Not knowing what she was drinking, she decided to sip it first. Simply a precaution.

Laura, on the other hand, downed it in one gulp.

"Go easy now," Laura warned after she coughed. "This stuff's got a kick."

Nightveil sipped the hearty liquor, felt it burn all the way down.

"Smooth," she said, adding a few extra *O*'s to drag out the word.

"That's some of my best hooch, you're drinking, sister," a husky voice said from behind the bar.

Nightveil turned and found herself once again staring into familiar eyes.

"Well there you are," Laura said with a flourish. "Mags, meet my new pal, Nightveil. Nightveil, meet Mags."

"Mags, huh?" Nightveil said, shaking hands with an older version of Laura Wright.

"What can I say? I never liked the name Laura. Plus, in a place like this it didn't seem to fit," Mags said, twirling a finger to encompass the room.

"Besides, I've always been a bit of a black sheep. Around here, being unique is an asset.

"I guess so," Nightveil said before changing the subject. "Nice place you have here."

"It's a dump," Mags said with a grin. "But it's my dump."

"Seems to be pretty popular, no matter how you look at it."

"I've been lucky." Mags pulled a glass and poured herself a shot of the same smooth amber liquid then refilled her guest's glasses as well. "This one's on the house, ladies."

"Thank you." Nightveil said.

"Much obliged, Mags," Laura said, tipping her glass slightly in salute.

"So, what brings you here, ladies?" Mags asked. "Don't tell me there's a Wright family reunion going on that I didn't hear about."

"Nothing so jovial," Laura said. "Our friend here is fighting herself a war and is recruiting."

Mags arched an eyebrow. "War? Who you fightin' with, girl?"

"Let's just say we wouldn't want her crashing our next reunion," Nightveil said.

"Another Laura Wright, huh?" Mags said. "What are the odds?"

"Gave me a headache just trying to do the math," Nightveil said.

"I'll bet. Why come to me?"

"Come on, Mags," Laura said. "You're the freakin' magic whisperer. If anybody can help her put the ki-bosh on our evil twin, it's you."

"Your faith in me is astounding," Mags said.

"But I'm not exactly what you'd call a fighter, not even when I was in my prime."

"Aw, who are you trying to fool, Mags? I've heard the stories."

"That's just what they are, kiddo. Stories," Mags said. "Only a tenth of them are even remotely close to the truth."

"I'll take that ten percent," Laura said.

"What about you?" Mags asked Nightveil.

Laura shrugged. "Until today, I didn't know either of you existed. I don't know your stories, but if you can help…"

Mags sighed, poured another drink, and downed it.

She looked from one version of her younger self to the other then sighed again.

"Tell me what's happening," Mags said.

And they did. Nightveil laid it all out for her, telling how she found bodies burned beyond recognition laying on the wasteland road. She told her about the evil Laura Wright who was planning to wipe them all out by collapsing the barrier between dimensions.

"This is bad," Mags said once Nightveil was finished.

"We know it's bad, Mags," Laura interrupted. "That's why we came to you."

Mags smiled. "You misunderstand me, kids. It's bad because we weren't expecting anyone to figure it all out so soon."

"Figure… out…" Laura mimicked, confused.

Nightveil's eyes widened.

"You're in on it with her," she muttered.

Mags' smile grew wider. "Smart girl."

Oh, crap!

One second later, all hell broke loose.

Two seconds after that, Nightveil found herself crashing through the bar's front window into oblivion.

11.

The Blue Bulleteer stepped through the breach.

And promptly threw up.

She had not expected the trip to churn up her insides as much as it did. Her new friend, the Laura Wright from another dimension who called herself Nightveil instead of Blue Bulleteer had told her that stepping through the breach would be no different than walking through a door from one room to another.

She was wrong.

Or she had lied.

Either way, the outcome was the same. The Blue Bulleteer dropped to all fours and puked her guts out all over the grass.

By the time she was empty and the nausea subsided, the Blue Bulleteer wiped the spittle from her lip with the back of her gloved hand and flung it away. She sat back easily on the soft grass beneath her, careful to avoid the foul smelling mush that had once been a meal. Now that she had time to look around, she realized that she was in a forest, or at the very least a wooded area. The pine trees told her that she was most likely in the south. She had been born in Florida and this place reminded her of her old home before she moved to New York to join the war effort.

Th sun was just rising to the east, the warm rays slowly burning off the cool morning dew that covered the shaded areas underneath the canopy of leaves. The smell of home was a warm remembrance until she reminded herself that this was not her home. Not really, even though the scents and sensations were the same.

Her home was still a dimensional breach away, under siege as it had been for the past eighty years. There was no time to sit around and enjoy this moment of peace.

Okay, so, if I was an all-powerful magician super-hero, where would I be? she wondered, looking skyward as clouds shown yellow and orange overhead from the morning sun.

The plan she had cooked up with Nightveil and Azagoth before she left her world had Blue Bulleteer going from dimension to dimension looking for other Laura Wrights who might be interested in helping them save the universe. From what she had said of their enemy, who was also another version of Laura Wright who had gone to the dark side, had amassed more power than she had ever heard of any one person being able to contain, much less control.

With a rendezvous plan in place, Nightveil had headed off to recruit others to their cause as well.

Azagoth's magic had her tethered to her home dimension, a precaution her newfound friend, Nightveil hadn't had when she arrived on their Earth. If her mentor's spell worked as it was supposed to, she would be able to call for help and Azagoth would pull her out of whatever dimension she was in and back to their headquarters. She had also made him promise to pull her back when their enemies attacked again. If there was one constant in her universe, it was that he Japanese would attack at dawn. She could not leave her home undefended against the enemy's next strafing run.

Azagoth's batting average was not perfect, but it was good enough that she trusted him to dive into the breach he opened. This breach was at ground level instead of a few thousand feet in the air. He promised that would make her exits easier than her doppelganger's arrival in their reality had been.

At least he was right about one thing. She had landed on solid ground.

Looks like there's nobody around, she thought.

Not knowing what to expect, she had been warned not to use her powers unless absolutely necessary. She had also put on a jumpsuit and gloves over her usual uniform. It felt odd. She was used to wearing a skimpy outfit that gave her a lot of freedom of mobility. The jumpsuit tugged at her with every move she made.

Complaining about the wardrobe change had done little good so she was determined to deal with it.

I wonder if it's been treated with Dr. Richards' super suit sealant? she wondered. The super suit sealant was an amazing invention that had allowed people with powers to have their suits adapt to their abilities. Her own powers played havoc on regular clothing. Thanks to the sealant, her costume was affected by her power the same way her cells were. That allowed the costume to grow with her.

Otherwise, all of her giantess exploits would take place with her in the nude.

She wasn't quite ready to fight crime *au natural* just yet.

Weighing the options, she decided to chance it.

All it took was a thought and a familiar tingle danced across her skin, the hairs standing at attention as her body began to grow and expand upward. She didn't fully understand how the power worked, but it had come in handy more times that she cared to count. Surprisingly, the suit expanded with her.

As she reached the height of the trees that surrounded her, she eased aside limbs, careful not to break any or push over any trees. She was there to get a looksee, not to announce her presence. At least not yet.

She peeked over the top of a group of trees.

The area was so green and quiet. She saw buildings off in the distance, a small town from the look of it. It had been so long since she had stepped foot outside of New York City that she had almost forgotten how peaceful country living could be.

That's when an explosion went off nearby.

She looked for the source of the big boom. It took a moment before her eyes focused on a squadron of flying craft that were making a run toward her position. They didn't look like planes or any type of aircraft she had ever seen. They reminded her of something she had seen at the pictures when she was a child. *Mission to Mars*, she recalled the title.

Those things are space ships!

As her mind raced through possible scenarios, Blue Bulleteer saw something else. The space ships were chasing a much smaller object.

A woman wearing an all-too familiar cape.

Nightveil!

The lead ship opened fire on the flying hero and the air filled with concussive force as the bomb exploded nearby. Nightveil managed to avoid the deadly attack, but the Blue Bulleteer held on to the trees to steady herself.

Well, the good news is I've found her, she thought, her mind racing with possible ways to help.

Thought and action were as one. As soon as the idea hit her, the Blue Bulleteer's power flared to life and she grew above the tree line, breaking through the leaves like a sea serpent rising up from the watery depths.

Nightveil saw her first and swerved to fly around the giant woman who suddenly appeared in her path.

The pilots of one of the ships panicked and the ship banked hard, crashing into one of his partners and destroying both ships in a massive explosion.

Two of the ships opened fire on the giant, but the Blue Bulleteer swatted them away easily and they exploded harmlessly in the upper atmosphere. A third fired and the missile detonated near her head, knocking her off balance.

The Blue Bulleteer kept her balance, but now she was angry.

She reached out and plucked the offending space ship out of the air as though it were nothing more than an annoying insect buzzing about her head. She threw the space ship to the ground hard, as if it were a football in desperate need of being spiked.

It hit the ground and cracked open, smoke pouring from the damaged hull.

"Who are you?" Nightveil shouted as she hovered near the Blue Bulleter's head.

"Just call me the cavalry," BB joked. "Let's take care of these guys and you and I can talk, what do you say?"

"Fine," Nightveil said and took off on an intercept course for one of the three remaining ships that bore down on them.

The ship opened fire with all of its weapons, bringing them to bear on Nightveil.

The Mystic Maid of Might stretched forth her hands and pink swirling bands formed around them and shielded her from the blast. Missiles exploded against the bands while the energy weapons fire was deflected away. It was an impressive display of the hero's prowess.

Blue Bulleteer increased her size again and swatted the nearest ship away with the back of her hand as though it were an annoying insect. The ship flipped end over end through the bright morning sky.

The ship tumbled out of the sky and crashed into a copse of trees before it exploded into a fiery mess. The surrounding trees ignited under whatever the aliens used as fuel, which burned blue, red, and purple. The fire threatened to spread as more trees and leaves went up in flames.

Blue Bulleteer cursed then kicked dirt in the

direction of the fire, smothering most of it under a wave of overturned topsoil. It didn't stop the fire, but it would slow it down.

Before she could do more, another ship came at her, breaking off its attack on Nighveil to take potshots at the giant. The pilot had learned from the mistakes made by his comrades. She made a grab for the ship, but the pilot took the ship into a hard left and avoided her grasp.

"Come here, you little bas..."

Missiles exploded near the Blue Bulleteer's head. Her ears were ringing as though they were playing the *Carol of the bells* that was a Christmas favorite of hers. Off balance, she took a step back, her heel catching on a fallen tree. Blue Bulleteer fell backward into the trees.

Acting on instinct, she began to shrink as he fell so as not to be impaled on any of the trees like spikes. The fall was going to hurt bad enough. Being stabbed was a kind of pain she did not need.

Above, Nightveil reached out with green bands that ensnared each of the last two remaining ships as though they were a lasso. The ships strained against the power that ensnared them. The more the struggled, the more intense the pressure on Nightveil's strength, both physical and mental.

"N... not to-today, pal," she muttered as sweat began to trickle down her face.

With a primal scream, Nightveil dug deep into her reserves and with a mighty heave, pulled both ships into one another where they crashed into one another seconds ahead of a welcome eruption that incinerated both ships.

Exhausted, Nightveil slowly dropped to the ground.

She landed next to the Blue Bulleteer.

"Well, that was fun," Blue Bulleteer joked, offering a pained chuckle.

"I've had worse workouts," Nightveil said. "Just usually not this early in the morning."

"I guess you're wondering who I am," Blue Bulleteer said.

Nightveil smirked. Hands defiantly on her hips, she gave the newcomer a closer look.

"Normally, that would be my first question," she said. "But I kinda already know the answer to that one. I'm guessing you're from... oh, shall we say, *out of town*?"

"Something like that," Blue Bulleteer said with a smile.

"Then, I guess the question I really have is, what do you want?"

"Straight to the point," Blue Bulleteer said. "I can appreciate that."

Several trucks had arrived on the scene and hazmat suited men and women rushed toward the downed spacecraft. A third truck arrived emblazoned with the F.E.M.Force logo on the side.

"Let's take a walk while your friends clean up the mess."

Nightveil signaled the team to give them some space. The woman in charge nodded and began directing her troops to action.

"It's been a bit of a hectic morning," Nightveil said. "I'm tired and could really use a hot bath and a massage after that." She motioned toward the busted up space ships lying nearby. "So, make it quick."

And she did. Blue Bulleteer laid it all out for her doppelganger. She explained the multiple alternate universes as they had been described to her, which turned out to be unnecessary. This Nightveil was not only aware of alternate realities, but had, herself, visited a few of them in the past. She was also familiar with the Crossroads of Infinity and the vortex at its center, though she was not aware of the evil Laura Wright who was even at that moment working to destroy it.

Once she was finished explaining, Blue Bulleteer looked at Nightveil.

"Will you help?" she asked.

Nightveil was silent a long moment and Laura was beginning to think that she would not help her.

"Who am I to turn away Laura Wright?" Nightveil asked with a hint of a grin.

"What do you need?"

12.

Nightveil's eyes shot open and she regretted the action immediately.

Panic nibbled at the recesses of her mind as she struggled to figure out where she was and how she got wherever that was. She tried to recall, in vivid detail, how she had come to find herself lying on a bed of glass in the dirt outside what looked like a two-bit dive bar in the middle of nowhere. That terrifying sense of not knowing tugged at her until her memory finally coalesced and it all came flooding back to her.

There was a barfight.

Maggie, the proprietor of the dive in question, had hit her with something. Hard. Nightveil wasn't sure exactly what she had been slugged with, but from the way her entire body ached, it felt like she had been hit by a fully loaded freight train barreling along at top speed.

She rolled over onto her side, moving slowly in a futile effort to lessen the pain. The hard-packed earth and glass that had once been the bar's window crunching beneath her as she moved ever so carefully. Small cuts covered her entire body, mostly from the shattered glass. The bar matron's punch that sent her flamin' near into orbit had popped a blood vessel in her nose and was sure to leave her bruised from head to toe in the morning, provided she lived that long.

The metallic tang of blood from her bleeding nose rolled over her lips and came in contact with her tongue.

She spat and the blood sizzled when it hit the ground. It reminded her of the wasteland where the ground was charged and ready to zap anyone who came in contact with it. Magic Maggie's Bar wasn't located in the wasteland, of that she was fairly certain, but it was nearby. Nightveil could practically feel the chaotic resonance on the wind.

To say that things were not going exactly to plan was a bit of an understatement.

She knew there was a risk in trying to round up additional Laura Wrights and sway them to her cause, but it seemed like a good solution to her very unique problem at the time. Now, she was less sure how good of a plan it really was or if they would even survive long enough to take the fight to the evil Nightveil who was intent on destroying the vortex at the Crossroads of Infinity.

Truthfully, she had never expected to encounter another "*bad*" Laura Wright out there. She had convinced herself that one bad apple out of the bunch was a one-off aberration, the exception that proved the rule that Laura Wright, no matter what she called herself, was one of the good guys.

The simple truth of the matter was that it had never occurred to her that there might be other versions of herself out there who would not only be sympathetic to the cause of the evil Laura Wright that she had faced off against on the wasteland path and lost, but that they would ally themselves with her against the rest of the cosmos. One was explainable, an anomaly, a lone aberration that defied explanation. She could chalk a lone instance up as... because alternate reality. But now, to find another sympathetic to her evil counterpart's evil scheme was a punch to the gut. It never occurred to her that there could be more than one Laura Wright to switch sides.

She was wrong.

And now she was paying the price for that mistake. Nightveil hurt so bad even her teeth ached.

Her error could possibly cost them the entire war if Maggie somehow managed to get word to the evil Laura before she was ready to face her again. For a moment, the thought of retreating seemed logical, if unappealing. The simple truth of the matter, whether it was a good idea or not, was that she was too far involved in this affair to turn back now. Retreat was not a viable option as far as she was concerned.

The enemy had to be stopped and it was her... their... duty to stop them. The best way to stop Laura Wright was with another Laura Wright.

Plans were already set in motion. Others were being recruited, even now. Despite the pain, she had to see the plan through to the end. It was, after all, her plan and she had an important part to play in it.

Ignoring the pain shooting through her muscles, Nightveil pushed herself off the hard-packed dirt and got back on unsteady feet.

Through the busted window, she could see that the bar, which had felt a bit tense since she arrived, had now erupted into full blown chaos. Being thrown through the bar's front window by the owner was all the spark it took to ignite the powder keg inside Magic Maggie's Bar.

Once the spark was lit, it quickly became a roaring inferno.

A magic barfight.

If not for the urgency of her mission, Nightveil might have enjoyed watching the mystics go at it like this, a mixture of mystic might combined with a good old fashioned hand to hand dust up. Things, however, were extremely urgent so there was no time to watch and learn.

Now, chaos reigned inside the bar.

Until Maximus the Mage knocked out the Arbiter of Chaos with a chair to the back of the head. The chair shattered into tiny fragments and Chaos dropped like a stone, crashing through a table on his way down.

Meanwhile, a strange bearded sorcerer she did not know threw bolts of energy at those who attacked him from the front while his cloak, kept the attackers from behind at bay by slapping at them as though it were a wet towel. Nightveil wondered if she could teach her own Cloak of Darkness to do something similar.

The fact that it was the bar's owner, a woman several years older than she that knocked Nightveil through the window like a ragdoll that really hurt the most sensitive spot of all, her pride.

Nightveil reflexively used a shield to deflect a flying chair that soared through the window straight toward her head. The chair effortlessly bounced off the shield, careening off into the unknown.

This is ridiculous! was all she could think as she watched the remaining magic users fire off attacks wildly at one another inside the dive bar. It was not something she ever expected to see. Magicians were supposed to be all about will power and self-control. Not so where these magic wielders were concerned. She wondered how long these aggressive feelings had been kept under wraps, just waiting for the right incident to erupt.

The bar was in shambles. Lights dangled from the ceiling, barely attached by a single chain. Furniture was broken with copious amounts of alcohol and broken glass spilled all over the floor. The battle spun out of control, with some of the mages taking the battle outside of the pocket dimension where this bar was located and back to their own dimensions. Nightveil had originally considered asking the assembled bar patrons to help with her quest, but she could see now that such an idea would have blown up in her face. Most of the bar's patrons were strangers, men and women she did not know and could not trust.

She was happy to see them leave.

One less problem to deal with.

There was no time to worry about it now, though. She needed answers and for that, she had to find Mags before the bar matron escaped and warned her partner that Nightveil was conspiring against her plans.

Near the bar, the depowered Laura Wright from another dimension held her own against the bartender. He was twice her size, but once she swatted him aside with the staff of Doominus Rex she kept clutched in her gloved right hand, he crumpled to the floor in an unconscious heap.

Laura leapt over the bar and headed for the back, shouting Maggie's name.

Nightveil's first instinct was to run around to the back of the bar and cut them off at the pass, but then she remembered that Magic Maggie's Bar sat on its own plane of existence, separated from all other pocket dimensions. Things like *around back* didn't mean much in a place where everything had been constructed to fit the architect's whim. Knowing what she now did about Magic Maggie, the back room could have easily been in another pocket dimension all its own for all any of them knew so cutting her of at the pass was not an option.

Guess we're taking the direct route then!

Nightveil leapt through the broken window and joined her traveling companion behind the bar. She ducked to avoid a tossed beer bottle and a broken chair before erecting a shield to defend against an energy attack from a half-blind wizard whose glasses had been knocked off his head in the melee. He was blindly throwing off spells in all directions and hoping they made contact.

"Where's Mags?" Nightveil shouted as the shield took another direct hit.

"That way!" Laura roared back, pointing toward the back room off the end of the bar. "She ducked in there!"

"Go!" Nightveil shouted. "We have to stop her before she gets away!"

Using the Doominus Rex, Laura swatted away

the bouncer with a single swing. A simple love tap demolished the door leading to the manager's office. She stepped inside the room with Nightveil following only a step behind.

Nightveil felt the hair on her arm stiffen as she crossed the threshold. It was as she suspected, the doorway not only went to another room, but that room was a pocket dimension within a pocket dimension. She had guessed correctly. Heading around back would not have worked at all.

Maggie stood alone in the room, her back to the far wall.

She was smiling.

"That can't be good," Nightveil muttered.

"It never is," Laura muttered.

Behind them, a new door slammed shut, locking them all inside together.

"Nope. Not good."

Before anyone could mutter a word, the room burst into eldritch flame all around them, burning green, purple, and red.

"Oh, I hate it when I'm right," Nightveil said, feeling the sweat immediately pop on her forehead even as her fingers began to dance around a spell to keep the flames at bay.

"So, little doppelgangers," Mags said menacingly. "You wanted me. Now that you have me, admit it, you kind of wish I had escaped, don't you?"

"Come on, Mags. You've known me a long time," Laura said, easing closer to the bartender. "We've hoisted many a pint together in this place. I thought we were friends. Talk to me. Tell me why you're doing this."

"What are you doing?" Nightveil asked.

"I'm trying to talk her down."

"You really think that's going to work?"

"Only one way to know for sure."

Laura took another non-threatening step closer. "Talk to me, Mags," she pleaded.

Nightveil moved to the other side of the room, careful to avoid the flames that climbed the walls. If talking didn't do the trick, and it seemed unlikely that it would, she would be in position for a flanking attack.

"You really want to know why?" Mags said, her raspy voice even tempered, unfazed by the flames she created.

"I think I'm entitled to some truth, don't you?"

Mags laughed. "You know, I used to think that too."

"What happened?"

"Someone told me the truth."

"And?"

"And here we are," Mags said, her laughter turning to tears. "This is what the truth gets you!"

"And where is this, Mags?" Laura pleaded. "Come on. It's not too late for you to help us. We can stop this. There's still time."

"No," Mags said softly, suddenly very interested in the floor. "The truth is what brought us here, Laura. I knew this moment would come. I've known it for a very long time, but I accepted it. I'm just sorry it had to be you."

"What're you…" Laura started.

Oh, crap, Nightveil thought.

Magic Maggie looked up, her eyes alight with radiant energy.

I hate it when I'm right!

Maggie smiled, a wide and terrifying visage that sent shivers down Nightveil's spine.

"Time's up."

Oh, damn.

Nightveil lunged at Mags, but she wasn't fast enough.

With a simple wave of her hand, Magic Maggie's Bar exploded.

13.

"Ouch."

Once again Nightveil found herself lying face first on the ground. She had lost track of how many times she had found herself knocked down since she first set foot on the sands of Daytona Beach. It seemed so long ago to her now, but less than a day had passed since her sojourn to the beach looking for fun and sun in the sand.

She looked left and right for any sign of her friend, Laura, but did not see her anywhere nearby. It was not difficult to get lost in these surroundings, Nightveil understood once she felt the familiar tingle where her extremities touched the ground.

Unlike the last time, this time she had no trouble recognizing her surroundings when she came to. This time, she was in the worst place she could possibly be.

"Oh, crap," she muttered.

She knew exactly where she found herself and that knowledge terrified her.

No! I'm not ready yet!

"The Wasteland," she muttered.

"Welcome back," a familiar voice called out from above. "I admit, I didn't think you had it in you to come back here and face me, much less all by your lonesome. Someone woke up with a sense of self-importance this morning."

Nightveil lifted her eyes skyward, anger seething in them.

Hovering above her was her evil counterpart.

Nightveil stared daggers at the woman named Laura Wright. This woman who had turned her back on the very code that she had lived by her entire adult life. On the day she received her powers, when the Blue Bulleteer became Nightveil, she saw how dangerous her newfound skills could be if improperly handled. She had been afraid then, as she remained today, afraid of what might happen if she were to misuse her power. The terror of what that issue might look like had led to many a sleepless night.

And now… now that nightmare hovered above her large as life.

No. Larger than life.

The Laura Wright who threatened to destroy all life as they knew it believed fully in her cause, just as Nightveil completely disagreed. For all the lives she was about to stamp out, Laura Wright still saw herself as the hero of her story.

Nightveil saw her greatest nightmare come to life. She wondered what it would take to push her over the edge like it had her other self? If she reached her breaking point, would Nightveil choose the same dark path toward destruction, death, and mayhem? She hoped not, but how could she know for sure? That uncertainty terrified her all the way down to her soul.

"Are you ready to end this charade, little one?" Laura Wright asked. Her voice was like honey, but the words dripped with venom.

"No time like the present, I suppose," Nightveil said before launching herself at her counterpart, spurred on by her anger. She was angry at her enemy, angry at herself, and angry at the circumstances that had set these events in motion.

Leading with her shoulder, she slammed into the evil woman with as much force as she could muster, knocking her foe off balance as intended. One of the benefits of being taught to fight by a warrior as skilled as Ms. Victory, who was one of the most naturally gifted fighters on the planet, was learning the little tricks she used to turn the tide in her favor. Nightveil had picked up more than a few of those tricks during their numerous sparring sessions over the years.

Ms. Victory did not like to lose.

Neither did Nightveil.

Energy formed around her hands like boxing gloves as Nightveil pressed her advantage. Like a prizefighter, she came out swinging, landing blow after blow against her enemy until her hand were nearly numb.

The enemy pushed her away and Nightveil tumbled end over end. Surprisingly, even to herself, she managed to remain aloft, coming to rest above the charred wasteland road.

"That the best you've got?" Nightveil shouted.

"Not even close. You came to face me alone in, what, honorable combat?"

Nightveil chuffed. "Looks that way, doesn't it?"

"Foolish girl. Your coming at me alone is the mystical equivalent of bringing a pocket knife to a tank battle."

"Now who's feeling self-important? Powerful, you may be, but it's still you and me. One on one, I'm thinking I like my odds."

The enemy smiled.

"You see, this is where you're mistaken. I never said I came alone."

The enemy stretched out her arms to the side as explosions of mystical energy danced around her limbs. She cackled with laughter as she quickly flung her arms above her head, fists clenched tight.

"And I don't do *honorable* combat."

Mystic bolts fired off in all directions, striking the wasteland.

The enemy looked down at her foe.

"I brought an army," she said, menace dripping off each word.

Before Nightveil could guess at her motivation, she caught a glimpse of movement out of the corner of her eye.

There was no one there.

Then she saw it again and fear immediately gripped her heart.

The charred bodies that littered the wasteland... the murdered victims of her enemy...

They started to move.

***

"Oh, crap!"

Nightveil's heart seized in her throat.

Before her, thousands of charred corpses got to their feet. The sound of popping and snapping bones accompanied by the tearing of burnt flesh surrounded Nightveil. It was the sound that a million nightmares were made of and it cut right through her.

This is not good, her mind screamed, trying to block out the noise.

She had to get away so she took to the sky. Nightveil hovered above the reach of the undead creatures that reached for her. She was vastly outnumbered, but retreat was not an option. If she didn't stop her evil doppelganger, it would be the end of all of them. She suspected that there wouldn't be room for more than one Laura Wright in the brave new world her evil counterpart planned to create out of the ashes of the multiverse.

It was earlier than she had planned, but the plan went out the window the moment evil Laura animated the charred bodies on the wasteland as her army. For all her bravado to the contrary, Nightveil realized that she could not handle this particular problem alone.

The call went out across the dimensional barriers.

It was a mystic call to arms.

Only one word.

Now!

She only hoped her troops were ready.

If not, it was up to her and her hammer-wielding ally to save the day on their own.

She did not like their odds.

Nightveil snapped back to reality as the masses beneath her surged upward, clawing at her, pulling at her cloak and shoes.

Her mental signal suddenly cut off.

She hoped it got through. She was about to be too busy to try again.

The charred remains flowed at her like a wave, crawling and scrambling atop one another like ants descending on some sweet treat dropped on the front lawn. Nightveil kicked away the monstrosity gripping her heels, losing one of the tall spiked shoes in the process as it fell away and was quickly swallowed up by the darkness below.

A force blast knocked away the beast holding onto her cloak. It laughed off the blast, unhurt, but it was enough to make it let go. A kick with her now bare foot was enough to send the creature flipping over backward before being swallowed up by the swirling mass of burnt bodies.

She rose higher, trying to stay out of the creatures' reach.

This is getting out of hand, she thought. "Laura!" she yelled, trying to find her erstwhile partner in the chaos that surrounded her.

"All alone, little one?" the evil Laura said. "No friends to help you out?"

Nightveil opened her mouth to retort, but the sound escaped her lungs as the next wave of moving dead slammed into her.

The wind knocked out of her, Nightveil was pushed along with the wave as hundreds of cracked and fried fingers clawed at her.

Come on! Come on!

Nightveil fought off her attackers, but the numbers were against her. Eventually, these creatures, many of whom had once also been named

Laura Wright, would overwhelm her and she would lose.

Come on! Where are you?

And that's when she heard it. It wasn't a physical voice, but a whisper against the back of her mind. Just one word.

Ready.

Do it! Nightveil responded. *Hurry!*

A rough hand grabbed her foot, a familiar electric tingle running along her muscles, making them twitch. She gasped and, her focus momentarily broken, was pulled downward into the midst of the savage horde.

Once again charred skin and bone pulled at her, tugging and scratching.

Nightveil struggled to free herself, but she was outweighed by sheer numbers.

As they dragged her under, she thought she heard someone scream her name, but the sound was quickly drowned out by the shrill howl of the dead all around her.

***

Laura felt helpless as she watched her new friend pulled under by the creatures they were fighting.

She pushed forward, swinging the only weapon at her disposal, the staff of Doominus Rex. She gripped it firmly on her right hand, which was covered by the Glove of Rex. Touching the staff without the glove carried big consequences, namely burnt flesh and intense pain. It was a mistake you only made once, as the ache in her hand reminded her daily.

Swinging the staff as hard as she could, Laura cleared a path by batting aside the ashen-black creatures that had once been human.

She was making good headway, pushing forward toward her new friend.

She knew she was close when she saw purple. Nightveil's cape. The sorceress from another dimension was still fighting against her attackers, but their numbers were more than enough to overwhelm her. She was buried beneath a mound of the beasts as they clawed at her.

"Get away from her!" Laura screamed as she brought the Doominus Rex down atop the beasts, crumbling one to dust and scattering the others.

It was just enough to free Nightveil's arm, allowing her to fire a bolt of emerald green force at the others, knocking them back until she had space to breathe.

"You okay?"

"I'm…" Nightveil started, but was then overcome with an uncontrollable coughing _**fit**_. She spit up blood and ash then wiped away the excess from her mouth with the back of her gloved hand.

"I'll live. Thanks to you," she said after a moment.

"So, where's this army of yours?" Laura asked. "We could use some back up!"

"I don't know!"

Nightveil shouted to be heard over the rising din around them. The roar of the angry vortex had grown. When added to the sound of the undead creatures the enemy had summoned forth, the noise was almost deafening.

"I sent out the call, but they haven't answered!"

"What do you mean they didn't answer?"

Nightveil shrugged.

"You mean to tell me we're on our own here?" Laura Wright did not seem too keen on that scenario.

"Looks that way!"

Laura muttered something unintelligible and it was quickly swallowed by the roar that surrounded them.

"You got a plan?" Laura asked.

Nightveil smiled painfully. "We fight!"

Laura nodded.

"We fight!"

14.

"We fight!"

Just a stone's throw from the Crossroads of Infinity, the two Laura Wright's stood back to back, ready to fight. They were surrounded on the Wasteland leading to the vortex that lives at the center of the Crossroads.

Their situation looked hopeless.

But they were prepared to fight until there was no fight left in them.

"Good luck," Nightveil told her unlikely companion, a powered down version of herself who possessed a strength of will unlike any Nightveil had seen before.

"Right back at ya," Laura said, smiling in spite of the danger surrounding them.

The charred horde, many of whom had also once been named Laura Wright before their untimely death at the hands of yet another Laura Wright, moved forward a step.

Both Laura's stood their ground, ready to spring into action. The plan had been for them to go into battle with an army backing them up, but something had stalled their arrival. Neither was certain they could win with just the two of them, but they were prepared to go down swinging.

Hands clenched into fists, Nightveil took a step

forward.

That's when they heard it.

It was soft, at first, little more than a whisper.

"Did you hear that?" Nightveil asked.

"I did," Laura said. "Is that…?"

Nightveil smiled. "Yes!"

She pointed to several bright flashes of light popping up all around the creatures that surrounded them.

"Looks like we've got company," Nightveil said.

A look flashed on the burnt faces of the undead horde. Was it surprise? She wasn't sure. Not that it mattered. The creatures sensed that victory, which had been so close only seconds ago, we beginning to ebb. The tide of battle was about to turn.

A large knife **_burst_** through the chest of the beast directly in front of Nightveil. The creature let out a dense *mewl* of astonishment before crumbling to ash right in front of her.

In its place stood a smiling Blue Bulleteer, holding the blade's hilt in her nimble fingers.

"Did you miss me?" the World War II era super-hero asked with a big smile full of incredibly perfect white teeth.

"You are a sight for sore eyes," Nightveil said. "Glad you could make it."

"Sorry, we're a bit late, but we had to wait on a couple of stragglers."

She motioned toward the various versions of Laura Wright that now stood on the wasteland, ready to fight their evil counterparts. Nightveil also noticed other familiar faces, men and women she had worked with before like Captain Paragon, Tara, Ms. Victory, the Scarlet Scorpion, Dragonfly, and more. Most were from other dimensions, other Earths. She wondered if her teammates on her plane of existence had also received the call. If so, Nightveil was certain they would have answered the call and been right there with her in the thick of things.

There were also those in the mix that she didn't recognize, but it mattered little. The arrival of Blue Bulleteer and her army was just the extra kick they needed to turn the tide of battle. She had saved the day... at least for the moment.

"No need for apologies, Laura," Nightveil said. "I'm just glad to see you!"

"Yeah. Better late than never," the depowered Laura said with a smile.

The Blue Bulleteer cast a sideways glance at the Laura Wright holding the Doominus Rex. "And who are you supposed to be?"

Laura smiled playfully. "I'm sure you can figure it out if you try, beautiful," she said playfully.

"How can you both be..." Blue Bulleteer started then shook her head. "Nevermind."

"We'll have time for meet 'n greets later," Nightveil interrupted. "Pick a partner and let's get this done!"

"Yes, ma'am," Blue Bulleteer said.

"And what are we supposed to do while they're fighting the troops?" Laura Wright asked, still holding firm to the staff of Doominus Rex.

Nightveil scanned the sky, trying to pick out her evil counterpart, the one responsible for creating the mess they were determined to clean up. The sky was filled with battle as various incarnations of Nightveil and her friends crisscrossed her vision like something out of a weird dream. On the one hand, it was awe-inspiring and just a touch strange to see so many versions of the same individuals sharing the same space.

So many of them sharing the same space for an extended period of time could have grave repercussions.

She needed to end things quick.

That meant finding…

"There she is!" Nightveil said when she spotted them.

Laura followed her gaze until she also saw their foes.

"We go after them," Nightveil said, pointing toward her evil counterpart and Magic Maggie. "We stop her and we stop this!"

"They're headed for the vortex!" Laura said.

"Go!" Blue Bulleteer shouted as she turned back toward the melee. "We've got this!"

"We're gone!"

Nightveil took to the sky and pulled her non-powered companion along with her, encasing her in an energy field to keep her aloft. She chanced a look over her shoulder and saw Blue Bulleteer grow into her giant form and wade into the fray.

"Tough chick," Laura said with a smile.

"You don't know the half of it," Nightveil said.

"So, uh, what exactly is the plan once we catch up with those two?"

"I'm working on it."

"That's not very reassuring."

"I imagine there will be a good deal of punching involved."

"Works for me," Laura said.

"Glad to hear it. They're almost to the vortex. I'm going to speed up. Hold one."

Laura tried, but the sudden acceleration made her feel as though she had left her stomach somewhere far behind them.

"You take care of Maggie," Nightveil said, pointing to the two women they were gaining on. "Her boss is mine."

"No problem."

***

At the edge of infinity, chaos reigned.

Just beyond the vortex's leading edge, Laura Wright hovered. She was the picture of calm as she stared straight into the heart of the vortex as if trying to understand its intricate purpose.

Then, she laughed.

"After all these years," she told Maggie, who hovered alongside her. "Years of study, of discipline, of sacrifice, have finally led me here. The source of the multiverse right here at my fingertips and it's mine for the taking. Mine!"

Tendrils of cosmic energy danced along the tips of her lithe, nimble fingers as she flexed them. Living bolts of lightning climbed up her wrist and forearm as if they had always been there.

The feeling was intoxicating.

Maggie almost said, "Don't you mean, *ours*?"

but then thought better of it. The deeper her friend embraced the dark magicks that now resided inside her, the less and less she resembled the woman she knew.

There was very little of the woman who wanted nothing more than to save the world from the evils that threatened to destroy it. Back then, when they first met, it was she who had been lost in Laura's world. Laura tried to help her return home, but she could not so she changed her name and died her hair so as not to confuse anyone with two Laura Wrights living on the same planet. On that day, Maggie Wright, Laura's "*sister*" was born.

Together, the Wright sisters protected their world, all the while not giving up on finding a way for Maggie to return home.

It took thirty years, but eventually, she did return to the realm of her birth.

Her Earth and the galaxy around it had been destroyed.

A bit of research revealed that it was a natural cataclysm, a cosmic '*hiccup*' that started a chain reaction that rent each world in that dimension to shreds, wiping out all life and leaving nothing but a vast dark empty void.

Maggie surrendered to her fate. Her world was gone. She would have to make peace with that fact and find a way to move forward from it and live. Eventually, she did just that.

Laura, however, found it impossible to move on.

She became obsessed with finding a way to restore her sister's dimension. Though nothing worked, Laura did discover that there were far more than just two dimensions at work. She discovered thousands upon thousands of dimensions, each varying by only the smallest of degrees. One small change created a new reality and weakened the whole, she believed.

At that moment, Laura's path was clear. She would remake the universe so there would only be one dimension, one Earth, and one Laura Wright.

And now, after all these years, Maggie suspected that the end was finally at hand.

Her sister had gotten her crisis.

The world was about to end.

And it was all her fault.

***

At the edge of infinity, chaos reigned.

Laura Wright's smile became a chuckle.

Then she laughed hard and loud.

"Isn't it exhilarating?" she shouted against the roar of the vortex.

Out of the corner of her eye, she saw them approach. The doppelgangers who thought they could stop her from saving the one true reality.

"You're too late, Nightveil," Laura shouted.

She snapped her fingers and a large ball of energy formed above her now opened hand. Plasmic energy bubbled and roiled beneath the pink energy barrier that supported it.

Laura knew Nightveil would understand what was about to happen.

"Say goodnight," Laura said before she sent the ball of dark energy toward the vortex. "You lose."

Nightveil and her gloved companion were too far away to stop the projectile. They were too late.

The multiverse… all of creation… was doomed.

15.

Nightveil screamed in defiance as she watched helpless as the mystic projectile zoomed toward its target. Never had she felt as helpless as she did in that moment. All she could do was stand by like a spectator and watch the multiverse end.

If only there were something I could...

Before she could complete the thought, her cloak began to move on its own, jerking her back and forth as though she were nothing but a puppet on a string. She tried to calm it, but the star-filled cloak grew more... well, agitated was the only word that seemed to fit. She couldn't understand it.

Within her cloak, the disturbance grew larger. Something was fighting to escape the confines of one of the myriad pocket universes hidden inside.

That's when she remembered her passenger.

So much had happened since she put the little creature there that she had almost forgotten about it. Laura eased open a portal that allowed the tiny vortex to emerge back into reality proper. The tiny cyclone still glowed green as it had on her Earth, but now that it was within close proximity to the larger vortex that spawned it, the green vortex began to move faster and faster now that it was back in its own realm. The tiny vortex bucked and heaved, fighting against the entrapment spell

Nightveil had placed around it.

It wanted to return home.

Who was she to deny it that one last request?

"What do we have to lose?" Nightveil said as she released the field and gave the vortex a push back toward where it belonged. It deserved to be reunited with the interdimensional vortex that surrounded the Crossroads of Infinity before the end came.

The vortex leapt free from her and crossed the gulf quickly, spinning at speeds nearly as fast as its chaotic larger brother. The vortex sped toward its home, catching and eventually passing the weapon tossed at the vortex by the evil Laura Wright.

Nightveil couldn't believe it.

The vortex twisted about and with a flick of its smallest aperture, send the plasmic bomb harmlessly off into the sky above the wasteland.

Suddenly, Nightveil felt hope return.

When the plasmic projectile exploded, the colors were swallowed up by the colorful blooms already filling the star-filled sky as if they were **_barely_** more than a momentary blip in the chaos. A moment before, this power was poised to destroy the multiverse. Now, it ended with a whimper like an insignificant pop of a flashbulb.

"No!" the evil villainous Laura Wright shouted as she watched her plan unravel. *It's not possible!* her mind screamed.

She knew who to blame.

She knew who was at fault.

And she spun around to face down her opponent.

"I'm going to kill y..." she started.

However, Nightveil was closer than she expected. Startled by her enemy's proximity, Laura recoiled slightly instead of throwing up a shield. That mistake cost her.

Nightveil punched her counterpart in the face.

The blow sent Laura reeling, falling end over end out of the sky toward the vortex. Laura dropped easily one hundred feet before stabilizing herself.

"It's over," Nightveil said as she dropped down to look her counterpart in the eyes. "Give up your mad scheme and we can all go home."

"Mad?" Laura screeched so she could be heard over the increasingly loud roar of the *vortex*. "My dear, you don't know the meaning of the word! I'm trying to save us!"

"By killing millions of people?"

Laura chuckled. "If you want to make an omelet..."

Before she could finish, Nightveil punched her again.

This time, she drew blood.

***

Magic Maggie barely sidestepped the attack.

Laura Wright came at her with the full force of the Doominus Rex staff she wielded. The mace at the end crackled with power. Depowered as she was, Laura was still a fierce fighter, but even she could only swing the heavy staff while wearing the bulky glove that allowed her to safely touch it for so long.

All Maggie had to do was stay out of her reach and she would prevail.

Maggie avoided the next staff attack. She was all too familiar with what would happen if it touched her. She was in no hurry to experience the kind of pain that the staff was reported to unleash.

Laura swung the staff at her again, but Maggie flew and up out of her reach. With no power of her own, Laura was airborne only because Nightveil held her there with her powers. Even while squaring off against Maggie's sister, Nightveil kept her partner aloft.

What she couldn't do was maneuver her through a fight.

Laura was basically locked in one spot high above the wasteland road. All Maggie had to do was keep a staff's length away and she could attack from afar.

Laura knocked away a blast with the staff. It was clumsy, but she held her own.

Maggie's second attack was wide and, instead of letting it go, Laura tried to block it as well. She stretched to her limit and when the blast struck the staff, it knocked it free from her gloved grip.

The staff of Doominus Rex tumbled as if in slow motion to the wasteland road below where it embedded itself in the dirt.

A howl filled the wasteland as soon as the staff penetrated. Combatants on both sides clasped their hands to their ears to try and block the terrifying sound.

Without the glove, Laura's only remaining defensive weapon was a gun, which she kept as a last resort. The glove of Doominus Rex would still come in handy, even without the staff. The glove was designed to channel powerful energy. It could be utilized like a shield against Maggie's magical attacks.

At least in theory. Laura had never had the opportunity for practical testing.

Instead, Maggie caught her off guard with a physical assault. She dropped down feet first and landed with her heels slamming into Laura's arm.

Laura yelped in pain, but managed to hold tight to the glove.

"Sorry it has to be like this," Maggie said as she pummeled Laura again and again. "I actually liked you! You were one of my favorite customers!"

I'm sorry too," Laura said as she wrapped her arms around her opponent, pinning her arms in place. "Nightveil! Drop the field!" she shouted, hoping her partner would hear her over the howling roar of the vortex.

When she felt the world fall out from beneath her, she knew that not only had she heard, but obeyed.

Laura and Maggie fell out of the sky together, a tangle of arms and legs intertwined.

They crashed into the wasteland hard, sending a shockwave across the desert floor.

When the dust settled, neither of them moved.

16.

At the edge of infinity, chaos reigned.

Nightveil squared off against her evil doppelganger just a stone's throw from the outer edge of the vortex. It was like fighting next to a category five tornado, the winds spinning at just under five hundred miles per hour. It was all she could do to hold her position as the vortex tugged at her, trying to pull her inside, which was the last place she wanted to go. The winds that made up the outer edge of the vortex were so strong they would most likely rip anything... or anyone who passed through them to shreds.

Getting ripped to shreds was not on her to do list today.

"Why are you doing this?" Nightveil asked.

"I have to save my universe."

"At the expense of all others?"

"Yes," Laura said.

"Why?"

Laura pointed toward the whirling vortex.

"This thing right here. It is the source of these new dimensions. This vortex cleaves off a small section of the prime dimension... the first dimension... my dimension! Those slivers are stolen from my dimension and then used to create a new, slightly altered dimension. My universe is weakened in the process."

"You can't really believe that, can you?" Nightveil pleaded. "Sure, there might be bleed over from time to time, but one dimension doesn't necessarily have anything to do with the other. It certainly doesn't weaken it! That's not how it works!"

"How foolishly naïve of you," Laura said. "I expected more from someone with your reputation. Have you not seen the chaos out there on the wasteland? Have you not yourself witnessed fractures between the dimensions? With each new divergence, all dimensions are diminished. My world has devolved into chaos. A monster sits on the throne, neighbors wage war where there used to be peace, men vs. women, black vs. white, it's all spinning out of control!"

"***And*** you think the vortex is responsible?"

"Yes!" Laura shouted. "I've examined all of the possibilities. This is the best solution! I need to make my people whole again!"

"What if you're wrong?" Nightveil pleaded. "What if some people are just... I don't know, bad... misguided... wrong?"

"It seems unlikely people's attitudes could shift so easily in so short of time," Laura said. "No. I know what is responsible and I must fix it."

"But what if you're wrong?" Nightveil repeated.

"Then I'm wrong," Laura said. "But I cannot take the chance. I have to do this."

Laura leapt toward the vortex.

Without a second thought, Nightveil chased after her.

She caught up with her doppelganger at the edge of the vortex, grabbing onto her in an effort to pull her away, but it was too late.

The vortex's gravity well grabbed them and pulled both Laura Wrights inside the vortex.

Their screams of agony echoed across the wasteland until even their voices were swallowed up by the vortex.

On the battlefield, the warriors from multiple dimensions froze at the sound. They lowered their weapons in a cease fire as all eyes turned to the great interdimensional vortex that surrounded the Crossroads of Infinity.

The fate of every dimension now rested in the hands of two women.

If they were still alive, that was.

***

At the center of infinity, chaos reigned.

Nightveil and Laura Wright rode the celestial winds like tiny ships tossed around at sea during a hurricane. Traveling at such speeds they should have been ripped apart, but a faint emerald glow surrounded them, protecting their soft, human bodies from the harsh gale force winds and galactic detritus that made up the vortex at the center of the Crossroads of Infinity.

All around them, images from multiple dimensions flashed past at blurred speed. She recognized some of the moments and players, but not all.

She watched as Blue Bulleteer led an army of

Amazonian warriors into battle on an alien world, surely a divergent reality very much different from her own.

Another flash showed her friend, Dragonfly saving civilians from an earthquake.

Still another flash showed a green planet explode into millions of tiny chunks as one lone rocket, too small to carry more than one person, blasted away only moment s before all life on the planet ended. Nightveil was there. She protected the rocket from the shockwave and sent it on its way toward a new home. She had no memory of this event either. Was it her future or another incarnation of Nightveil?

Other flashes of reality sped past. She saw multiple versions of F.E.M.Force and the Champions of Justice, with different members, some known and others a mystery to her. She was proud to know that so many Earths were protected by heroes willing to put themselves on the line to keep the planet safe.

She watched as a meteor the size of Texas sped toward her home planet only to be intercepted by a caped hero she did not recognize. The young woman smiled before punching the meteor repeatedly until it shattered into tiny rocks that could safely burn up on atmospheric entry.

Nightveil shut her eyes hard. The images were coming to fast for her to keep up. Combined with the roaring wind, the flashes threatened to overwhelm her. She succumbed to the darkness and drifted off into dreamless sleep.

Slowly, Nightveil opened her eyes.

"Ouch," she muttered, her voice barely above a pained whisper. Ever fiber of her being hurt from head to toe and every which way in between. She didn't know how long she had been out, not that time meant much inside the Crossroads of Infinity.

Passage through the vortex wall was unheard of, as far as she could recall. She remembered Azagoth telling her stories about those foolish enough to think they could ride the winds to the center of infinity in search of the unspeakable rewards that were rumored to reside there. Some thought it was money. Others believed it was unlimited power.

Nightveil had always believed that the only thing passage through the great barrier brought was a brutal, devastating death.

Apparently, she was wrong.

"Are we dead?" she asked.

"Apparently not."

Nightveil shifted her weight and rolled onto her side so she could see her foe, careful not to get slapped in the face by her billowing cape.

"Not what you were expecting, I take it?"

"No," Laura said. "It doesn't change anything though. To save my universe, I will destroy this place."

"You'll have to go through me first."

"That can be arranged."

"*I think not*," a third voice said, booming and echoing all around them as the roar of the vortex and accompanying wind storm ceased, surrounding them in warm, white light. "*There is no further need for violence*," the soothing voice said.

"Who are you?" Laura shrieked.

"*I am Infinity*," the voice said. "*You are now inside that which is me.*"

"Bullshit!" Laura spat. "The vortex is not alive!"

"I wouldn't put money on that," Nightveil muttered.

"*The vortex is only the shell that surrounds infinity*," the voice said. "*I am the living heart of the multiverse. Infinity is the beginning and ending of all life as you know it.*"

"So, you're the one making new dimensions?"

"*Yes. All dimensional planes are born here. I am mother… I am father… I am Infinity.*"

"You're destroying my dimension!"

"*No. I am not.*"

"Lies! I have seen the truth with my own eyes!" Laura shouted, tears streaming down her face. "You have been using my dimension to build the others, weakening us!"

"*You have been deceived, Laura Wright. All newly birthed dimensions are pulled directly from infinity… from me.*"

"I don't believe you!"

"Why won't you listen?" Nightveil pleaded.

"Because I know I'm right!"

Lashing out wildly, Laura threw a massive barrage of mystical bolts into the light.

Nothing happened.

"Stand down!" Nightveil said, grabbing and pinning her enemy's arms behind her back.

"Never!"

"*Perhaps you would like to see what life would be like if you are successful?*" Infinity said. There was less echo now, as though it was trying to whisper.

"Can you do that?" Nightveil asked.

"*Of course. That would be another divergent reality, after all. It too would be born from this place.*"

"My God…" Nightveil started.

The brightness intensified to the point it burned.

And suddenly, they were somewhere else.

17.

At the end of the world, serenity reigned.

Nightveil hadn't known what to expect when Infinity offered to show them a reality where Laura's crazy plan succeeded.

This wasn't it.

She and Laura Wright stood on a polished white floor so shiny they could see their reflections in the floor. All around them was stark white, no variations of color, smell, sound, or any sensation they had ever experienced.

It was as silent as the grave.

With each step, their heels thudded loudly, the only sound in the entire universe. It was all gone. Nothing had survived.

"This can't be right," Laura said.

"What did you think was going to happen?"

"I thought the dimensions would merge, become one again. I thought we could start over and do it right this time."

"It doesn't work like that," Nightveil said. "You know that. Some of our history has to be the same. Surely, you have seen some of the amazing things I have seen, traveled to so many remarkable new places that even Jean Luc Picard would be envious. The multiverse is vast and unique. It is filled with wonders more daring than even I could dream."

Nightveil pointed off into the nothingness than surrounded them.

"And you destroyed it," she said, somber. "Wiped the slate clean."

"This… this is not what I intended," Laura said. "This is not what I wanted!"

"Come on, Laura. You know as well as I do that there is one indisputable truth: magic always comes at a price."

Laura nodded, a tear rolling down her cheek.

"Is this a price you're ready to pay?"

"No."

"*But you have paid it, Laura Wright,*" Infinity said, the voice once more a booming echo. "*You chose to live here.*"

"It's not too late," Nightveil shouted. "Now that she knows, now that we know, we can prevent this eventuality from happening!"

"*I'm afraid, it is not that simple, Miss Wright.*"

"Somehow, I knew you were going to say that."

"*This place where you now reside is not an illusion. It is a true divergence, a new dimensional reality spun off from your own. This is the reality where your plan succeeded and the vortex was destroyed, thereby also destroying me.*"

"Wait," Nightveil said, confused. "How can you create a dimension if you were killed to create the divergence."

"*You see the paradox,*" Infinity said with what sounded like a nervous chuckle. "*A sacrifice had to be made to make this dimension possible. I am at a… loss to explain it.*"

"A sacrifice? Does that sacrifice have to be

you?"

"*I do not understand.*"

"What if I took your place?" Nightveil offered. "Let me be the sacrifice in your place and Infinity won't have to end here."

"*Why would you willingly end your life?*"

"Compared to the billions upon billions of lives that would be wiped out if you were destroyed, my life is rather insignificant," Nightveil said. "Don't make me break out the *needs of the many...* speech."

"*The needs...*"

"Let me to put it another way, I'm their protector. It's my job to keep them safe."

"It's my job too," Laura Wright said. "Or, at least it used to be."

Nightveil shot her a dirty look. "Oh, I think you've done just about enough, thank you."

Laura turned toward the light. "I caused this! Let me be the one to put it right!"

"*You realize what will happen, do you not?*"

"I do."

"*Very well, Laura Wright. Prepare yourself.*"

Nightveil stepped forward. "Now wait just a da..."

With a brilliant flash of light, they were gone.

***

At the edge of infinity, chaos reigned.

Laura Wright opened her eyes, not surprised to find herself once more outside the vortex. Nightveil was not there and she wondered for a moment if the disembodied voice had lied to her.

Then she started falling toward the great barrier and this time she understood that there would be no safe passage granted to the other side.

"Hang on!"

Laura turned toward the sound. She smiled as she saw Maggie heading toward her, intent on catching her, saving her. She and Maggie had been through so much together since they met. Even when she turned her back on everything she had once stood for, Maggie was there. Maggie always had her back, no matter what.

Maggie was the best thing that had ever happened to her.

And now Maggie was going to die trying to save her.

"No! Go back!" Laura shouted, but her voice was lost in the roar of the vortex barrier.

And then her sister was at her side.

"I got ya," Maggie said, using her magicks to pull them away from the barrier. "Let's get out of here!"

"I… can't," Laura said, trying to push her sister away. "I have to go into the barrier!"

"It's over," Maggie said softly. "We lost. Let's just go home."

"I can't," Laura said. "This is home now."

"Then it's my home, too, sis."

"No…"

"Where you go, I go, remember?"

With a smile and a snap of her finger, Maggie's magic faded.

The sisters held tight to one another as they fell into the vortex barrier and vanished.

Seconds later, the vortex exploded.

18.

At the edge of infinity, spring was in bloom.

Nightveil opened her eyes and squinted at the sunshine in her eyes. For a moment, she thought she was still lying on a sunny beach in Daytona, enjoying the final days of spring before Florida's brutally hot summer began in earnest.

However, it was not the coarseness of wet, sun-bleached sand she felt beneath her.

She sat up, surprised to find herself sitting on a field of soft grass, with wild flowers blooming all around.

"Where the hell am I?"

She looked left then right and smiled when she saw a familiar sight.

The vortex at the Crossroads of Infinity spun in the distance. Instead of the usual roar, the winds were quieter, more serene. Explosions of color no longer exploded overhead. Now, they were simply there, moving in a rhythm that put her at ease.

"I'm on the wasteland," Nightveil said, surprised to find that there were no electric shocks where she touched the ground.

She stood, dusted flower petals off her clothes, and looked around.

She was alone.

None of the other Laura Wrights were anywhere

to be seen. Also, none of the charred remains of her doppelganger's victims remained.

"What happened?" she asked, not expecting an answer.

"*All is once again as it was,*" the voice of Infinity said. "*The multiverse has been saved and Infinity is at peace for the first time in millennia and we have you to thank for it.*"

"I think you've got the wrong Laura Wright."

"*Nonsense. It was you who stood between your other self. It was also you who changed her mind. You opened her up to beliefs she had long since forgotten.*"

"Too bad she had to die."

"*What makes you think she is dead?*"

"You said there had to be a sacrifice?"

"*I did and there was. Laura Wright and her sister sacrificed themselves to save their universe and now... now there is a divergent reality where they were successful.*"

"Are you saying they're both alive?"

"*Yes. They are alive and well in their new altered reality. They are its protectors.*"

Nightveil smiled. It was the best result, but not one she expected to happen.

"Thank you," she said.

"*For what?*"

"For helping them."

"*You misunderstand, Miss Wright. I did not do this for them.*"

"Oh?"

"*No. I did it for you.*"

***

Repairs to Magic Maggie's bar were proceeded apace.

The new owner wasted no time hiring the best mystical construction firm she could find and put them to work sprucing the place up for the new grand re-opening. She was just putting the final personal touch over the bar when she heard the bell above the front door jingle.

"I love what you've done with the place," the newcomer said.

"Thanks," Laura Wright said as she climbed down off the ladder.

"Nice touch," Nightveil said, pointing toward the new decoration as she took a seat at the bar.

The staff of Doominus Rex hung over the bar, secured in place by a biometric locking system so no one could steal it, but keyed to the owner's unique bio-signature so it could be taken down in an instant if trouble reared its ugly head. The glove of Doominus Rex held a place of honor on a post closer to eye level, but also easily accessible.

"It really livens up the place, don't you think?"

"It gives it just the right ambiance," Nightveil joked.

"Yeah. Really classes up the joint."

They laughed.

"Looks like everything's coming together nicely, although I never really pictured you as a bartender."

"It's a living," Laura said as she plopped two glasses down on the freshly polished bar top.

"I can't stay long," Nightveil said.

"Oh?" Laura raised an eyebrow. "Hot date?"

"Something like that."

"Well, just one for the road then."

"One for the road."

Laura poured a drink for each of them and they clinked glasses.

"What shall we drink to?" Laura asked.

"To the bar," Nightveil said. "And hot dates."

"I'll drink to that."

Laura downed her drink in one shot.

Nightveil sipped at hers.

"You planning to change the name?" she asked.

Laura sat down her empty glass. "I was thinking about it, but there's a history to this place. Plus, there's already a perfectly good sign out there so why not keep it. Besides, I like the name. Magic Maggie's. Has a nice ring to it, don't you think?"

"Indeed, it does," Nightveil said as she stood and fished in her cloak for some cash.

"Oh, no," Laura said. "Your money's no good here, sister. You just promise to come back every now and then for a visit."

"Count on it," Nightveil said with a smile.

"Next time, I might even bring some friends with me," Nightveil said on the way out the door. "I think they would like it too."

"What's not to like?" Laura said with pride.

"Not a thing."

19.

It was a beautiful spring day in Daytona Beach, Florida.

As usual, the sands were full of revelers, party animals enjoying spring break and all the parties that went along with it. Bare-chested men and bikini-clad women moved like waves from one boardwalk to the next, enjoying the warm sand beneath their feet and the salty sea air.

The only one on the beach who did not seem to be enjoying himself was Pete Hall.

Pete wasn't just another beach bum, he was a man on a mission. It had been a couple of days since he met the most amazing woman right here on this very beach.

Then he almost drowned.

He wasn't too certain of the details, but the nurse at the hospital where he woke up the day before told him he had almost drowned and was saved when a woman pulled him from the ocean after a storm rolled in quickly.

The only thing Pete could remember about that day was seeing some dark clouds on the horizon and the beautiful eyes of the woman he had met.

Her name was Laura, Laura Wright.

And now she was gone.

He had spent the past two days wandering the

beaches, shops, and bars looking for her, but without any luck. She was gone and he had no idea what to do next. Even his friends had abandoned him to his mad search while they went off to party with some college girls they had met at a mixer the night before.

Finally, he realized that his was a fool's errand. The odds of finding one woman in a sea of thousands was nigh on impossible. He was ready to throw in the towel and try to forget about her, a task that he already knew would require a lot of alcohol by volume and at least three pretty co-eds.

So lost in thought was he, that Pete did not hear the shouted "Watch out!" until it was too late.

Something hit him in the back then fell away.

"Hey!" he shouted, but then smiled when he saw the fluorescent yellow frisbee lying on the sand next to him.

"A little help?" someone called from behind him.

Pete picked up the toy and was ready to send it sailing back to its owner when he finally caught sight of her.

A grinning Laura Wright walked toward him. Barefoot and wearing a green and yellow two-piece bikini, her hair in a ponytail, bouncing with each step, Laura approached with open arms.

"You planning to throw that thing?" she finally asked.

"What?" Pete fumbled.

Laura pointed at the frisbee in his hand.

"Oh, yeah. Right," Pete said clumsily.

He tossed the toy the short distance between

them and she caught it easily.

"I'm glad I ran into you," he said as she walked closer.

"Me too," she said with a tiny laugh. "It's been too long since somebody knocked me off my feet."

Pete actually blushed, which only endeared him to her more.

"I didn't think I'd ever see you again," he said.

"Never say never, Pete. That's my motto."

"And a good one it is too. What say you and I go grab a drink?"

Laura demurred slightly. "Actually, I've been having an odd week. If it's all the same to you, can we walk on the beach for a while?"

"Whatever you want, Laura. Whatever you want."

Laura Wright was having an odd day, but she realized that odd days weren't necessarily a bad thing and she planned to enjoy every single odd day he could.

The End.

ABOUT THE AUTHOR

Award-winning Author Bobby Nash has been in love with the character of Nightveil ever since he first read her adventures in AC Comics back in the late 1980's when he was in high school and only had dreams of writing comics for a living. This love affair continued for many years, but was one-sided as Bobby's attempts to pitch Nightveil stories to the publisher proved unsuccessful. Undeterred, Bobby continued to write until one day, Pro Se Productions' head honcho Tommy Hancock uttered the words that Bobby had been waiting over twenty years to hear. "We're going to be doing AC Comics novels," Tommy said on a panel at a con to which Bobby jumped in with "I call dibs on Nightveil!" This digest novel marks off a bucket list item and is definitely a dream come true for the author. Who knows, maybe Nightveil and company will invite him back to do it again. Bobby also writes other stuff you might also enjoy. Learn more about them at www.bobbynash.com and www.ben-books.com.

Made in the USA
Columbia, SC
07 March 2022

57273421R00107